NEVER LET ME GO

Joan Smith

NEVER LET ME GO

WHEELER
PUBLISHING, INC.
ROCKLAND, MA

★ AN AMERICAN COMPANY ★

Published in Large Print by arrangement with Ballantine Books, a division of Random House, Inc. in the United States and Canada

Wheeler Large Print Book Series.

Set in 16 pt Plantin.

Library of Congress Cataloging-in-Publication Data

Smith, Joan
    Never let me go / Joan Smith.
        p. (large print) cm.(Wheeler large print book series)
    ISBN 1-56895-514-6 (softcover)
    1. Women novelists—fiction. 2. Large type books.
I. Title. II. Series
[PR9199.3S55157N48 1997]
813'.54—dc21   97-32440
                                                                CIP

NEVER LET ME GO

Chapter One

Good friend for Jesus sake forbeare
To digg the dust encloased heare;
Blest be ye man yet spares thes stones
And curst be he yet moves my bones.

I stood on the north side of the chancel of Holy Trinity Church in Stratford-upon-Avon, gazing at the slab of stone bearing this bit of doggerel. Beneath the stone lay the dust of the world's greatest playwright, William Shakespeare. By legend, the words are his own, and I found it passing strange that he, who had put such marvels of poetry into the mouths of his characters, should have done so poorly by himself. Yet the simple warning sent a tremble quivering up my spine.

I was moved, but I had no premonition that before many days, I would be digging up the bones of a long dead lady myself, that I was already set on a course that would irrevocably change my perceptions, and my life. When I look back on it all, though, it is that moment by Shakespeare's grave that I see as the beginning.

I had come to England to escape the memory of a death, yet I found myself strangely drawn to graves and graveyards. I called the visit a research trip, but in truth

1

I was running away from the empty house where I had lived with my widowed father. For the three months since his death, I had sat at my word processor with no spark of an idea for my next historical novel. So when my April royalty check arrived, I grabbed it and ran away to lick my wounds, hoping England would inspire me.

My new book had a title, *Rebel Heart*, and a setting: seventeenth-century England during Cromwell's reign. The rebel heart beat in the breast of a Puritan daughter of one of Cromwell's officers. The Royalist who caused her to rebel against faith and father was the problem. I could not visualize him. He had no face, no name, no character or personality, no virtues or vices. Perhaps I had come to England to find him.

I had come to Stratford on a tour bus. When the group began wandering back to the bus, I went along with them, hurrying to get a window seat. The scenery was enchanting as the bus spirited us along. Sun glinted off the water; at the end of April the air already held the gentle warmth of summer.

When my seat-mate, Ellie Duncan, a retired schoolteacher from Ohio, suggested we open the window, I agreed. The unfurling leaves of lime trees formed a lacy umbrella of translucent green as the sunlight poured over them, dappling the roadway with shivering shadows. I breathed in the balmy air and gazed at the passing scene. Stratford had been exactly as I anticipated. Interesting, quaint, but not terribly exciting. The place where my heart beat faster had been at Shakespeare's grave. One thinks of the grave as final, the last stop. Death is not always the end, however. As I was to learn, it can even be a beginning.

I felt a sharp jab at my elbow. "Look at that!" Ellie exclaimed. "Our bus nearly hit that dog. The driver didn't even honk the horn."

I craned my head out the window. We had slowed down to turn the corner, but I didn't see the endangered dog. It seemed wrong, driving on the left side of the road. When the motorcycle came around the corner, I was afraid we would run into it. It was a black Harley, and the driver wore a helmet with a mask covering his face. He looked like some evil android. He turned to look at me, with my head craned out of the window. Perhaps he thought I was trying to call to him. His machine swerved dangerously toward us and nearly collided. I uttered one sharp, instinctive yelp of fear, then he was safely past, and the bus continued on.

"I wonder if he's an American," Ellie said. "He doesn't seem to be used to driving on the left."

Ellie and I had struck up one of those unlikely friendships that occur between people who have little in common, but are thrown together for a few days during trav-

3

el. She was a comfortable grandmother in her sixties; I was a working woman less than half her age. Maturity brings a sort of compassion, and at that time I enjoyed her company more than that of younger people.

"I expect you'll rent a car when we reach the New Forest," she said. "Isn't that where you'll be staying?"

"Yes, I saw a real estate agent's ad in a travel magazine. She's trying to find me a cottage to rent for a few months."

"Maybe you'll get started on your new novel," Ellie said. I had confided my problem to Ellie, which is strange, because I hadn't told my closer friends about my writer's block.

"I think the change of scene will be a big help."

"There's so much history here, isn't there?" Ellie said. "Every little village has some historical home or museum. And we've had three days of sunshine. I'm looking forward to one of their pea soupers."

Between the scenery and Ellie's easy company, the trip passed quickly. We took our parting at Southampton, promising to keep in touch. At the bus stop, I looked around for the estate agent, Mrs. Romero, who was supposed to meet me. There was only one woman waiting, and she didn't look like a Mrs. Romero. I was expecting a dark-haired Latin type. The woman standing on the curb had a halo of frizzy Titian hair, a wide, pink map-of-Ireland face, and green eyes. She was built like a pumpkin on pegs, and wore a loose-fitting flowered dress.

"Miss Savage?" she said, bustling forward.

"Yes. You're Mrs. Romero?"

We shook hands. "Call me Mollie," she said. "I'm Irish, as you might have guessed. Romero's my married name. Miguel loped off on me a dozen years ago. Good riddance, say I, the shiftless bounder. I've got my car double-parked in front of the greengrocer, so we'd best scoot before the law finds me out." She peered at her car, which was in no imminent danger of getting a ticket.

She took up one of my cases, I took the other, and we crossed the road to the beat-up white Morris Mini double-parked in front of the greengrocer's shop. The car hardly looked big enough to hold her, let alone myself and two substantial pieces of luggage, but we managed to get bags and bodies stowed. The engine spluttered, and finally lurched away from the curb.

To put it kindly, Mollie was an inexpert driver. Until we were out of the city and driving through the lush countryside, it seemed best not to distract her with conversation.

When we hit a quiet spot on the road she said, "I've found just the place for you, dear, a little cottage in Lyndhurst, the Queen Town of the New Forest. Two beds, modern plumbing, and a bit of a garden at the back. It's a lovely town, all kinds of arts and crafts and lots of pubs."

We drove into a town that did look very pretty, and just as she described. The buildings were ancient but well preserved. Some of the houses had thatch roofs. But when she took me to the cottage, I was disappointed to see it was just a modern little brick bungalow. I had been picturing something quainter. She read the disappointment on my face.

"I thought, you being American and all, you'd want your modern conveniences," she said. Her green eyes twinkled with something akin to mischief.

"It's very nice, but I pictured an older cottage, with maybe a thatched roof, or... I don't know. Just something older and more picturesque. Of course, I do want running water and a flush toilet."

"I know exactly the place you'd love. Quaint, but it's been modernized a bit. Unfortunately..."

"Somebody beat me to it, huh?"

"Devil a bit of it!" she said, and laughed merrily. "I can't unload it for love or money."

"What's the matter with it? Is it haunted?" I asked eagerly. I had been hearing of ghosts in a few tours of the stately homes of England.

"Worse. It's on the grounds of Chêne Bay. One of those rock-and-roll fellows bought up the entire estate. A grand old place with stables, a lake—all the extras. He'll make a shambles of it, I expect. The group calls itself Roarshock, and that's just what their

6

music is. A shocking roar. They're what you call punk rockers. It's just the head honcho who lives there. He calls himself Ivan the Terrible. He isn't so bad if you can get past the purple spiked hair and the hardware hanging off his ears and the pin in his nose. He tells me his dad is a vicar, and his uncle teaches at Oxford. Quite a good family really. Can you beat that?" she said, and laughed.

"A rebel without a cause. Is the cottage close to the house?"

"There's a quarter of a mile separating them. Ivan isn't around much. He has a recording studio in London. Some of his friends are using the house to make a video at the moment. The movie crew seem quite decent. You'll see more short-haired businessmen around than anything else. Agents and such."

"Let's have a look at the cottage," I said, and we squeezed back into the Mini.

"It's just a mile beyond Lyndhurst. Actually an ideal location, a bit away from the town, but close enough to come into the pubs and flicks if you want company."

She chatted on about the New Forest as we drove to the cottage. "They call it the New Forest, but it's actually as old as the hills. William the Conqueror is the one who set it up as a hunting ground for himself. Nice to be king, eh? Part of it's privately owned. The ponies you hear about are called wild, but they all belong to people. If you see one wandering the street, don't

7

get any ideas about putting a saddle on it."

The road was narrow and twisty—crinkum-crankum, Mollie called it. She nearly ran over a goose that had wandered into her path. Other than that, the drive was uneventful. In some places, the old forest grew right up to the road's edge; at others we had a view of meadows spangled with wildflowers. A few small, old cottages dotted the roadside, their privacy protected by those strips of mini forests the English call hedgerows. We didn't see any ponies.

"That's Chêne Bay ahead," she said, when we'd been driving for what seemed longer than a mile. Maybe it was the jiggling car or the poor roadway that caused it, or just that so many interesting things were squeezed into a short space.

I peered through the windshield to an ancient heap of gray stone perched atop a low rise. The house was done in the Palladian style with a classical portico and a dome on top. An incredibly green park, spotted with trees, ran gracefully down to the roadway. Sunlight sparkled off a winding snake of water meandering through the park. Mollie turned in at an iron gate. About a quarter of a mile farther up the rise stood Chêne Bay. She turned right almost immediately into a dirt road and parked in front of a stand of hornbeam and yews. We got out and went along to an opening in the bush.

"This is it," she said. "Chêne Mow. Pretty, isn't it?"

It wasn't half-timbered, or thatched, or any of the things I had been thinking I wanted. But it was perfect. A perfect little English cottage, built of flint with a slate roof that gleamed with a dull iridescence in the sunlight, like a pigeon's back. Bloodred roses climbed up the walls; the oaken door was rounded at the top and had a big lion's-head knocker. Latticed windows twinkled a welcome in the sunlight.

"I'll take it," I said, before we even went inside. The speed of my decision surprised both Mollie and me. The minute I laid an eye on that cottage, I knew it was perfect for me. It felt like home. I liked the location, away from the city, and the privacy of it, crouching behind the hedge.

Mollie gave me a sharp, conning look. "I knew you would," she said. "I can always tell."

"Nothing like experience. You recognized me for a romantic."

"Oh no, dear. It's not the experience. I just know these things. I'm a psychic. Did I mention it?"

Chapter Two

When a twentieth-century businesswoman suddenly announces she's read your mind, the instinctive reaction is doubt. I smiled politely and murmured something non-committal. Mollie's wide pink face was smiling, too, but the green eyes showed a touch of flint.

"But you aren't interested in that," she said. "Let's go in and see the house."

"Yes, I am!" I exclaimed, when I saw she was serious. I had planned to look into the hidden corners and crannies of England while I was here, and talk to some of the more outrageous eccentrics, but I hadn't expected to be handed one on a platter. "I'd like to hear all about it, Mollie."

"We'll see," she said over her shoulder. Already her flowered dress was billowing its way toward the rounded oaken doorway. Her pink spike heels rammed into the earth between the cobblestones, impeding her progress. Sunlight struck the orange frizz of her hair, turning it into a halo.

I admired the roses as she struggled with the big brass key, then followed her into the house. The windows that twinkled so brightly in the sunlight were small, and inadequate to the job of illuminating the house. She flicked on the lights, and a quaint sitting room that might have come from a Grimms' fairy-tale illustration sprang into view. It was whitewashed, with dark beams. The pegged floor was partially covered by a braided rug. A big fireplace with black andirons and firedogs was the focal point of the room.

On a chilly evening, I'd light the fire and

10

toss cushions on the floor to enjoy the blaze. The furnishings were old and dark and too large for the room, but the black corduroy sofa was newish. A bookcase filled with smoke-darkened books stood below the windows. There were a couple of undistinguished old paintings on the wall, a cheap stereo and TV set.

The rest of the downstairs consisted of a small dining room and a kitchen that might have come off the ark. The sink, as far as I could tell, was made of stone. The countertops were wood with red linoleum nailed down roughly on top. The floor was covered with the same liver red linoleum. But the kitchen had cupboards with bright, mismatched dishes behind glass doors, and an electric stove of ancient vintage.

Mollie peered to see how an American, with our well-known love of modern cons, took to this primitive room. "It's not so bad," I said. At least it was clean. "I'm looking forward to foraging for veggies and herbs in the garden out back."

Mollie gave me a very queer look. "You mentioned a garden," I said. Imagination had done the rest. I pictured an old-style knot garden. I could almost smell the sage and thyme.

"That was the other house, Belle. But this place has a garden, too. Shall we go upstairs?"

I turned left and opened a plain wooden slab door on to a dark, narrow stairway.

"That's right, dear. Just go along up those stairs," Mollie said. "Best leave the door open. It's dark."

Enough light came from both below and above to show rough plastered walls and uncarpeted stairs. She didn't ask me how I knew that door led to the stairs, but I felt she must be curious. "I didn't see any stairs in the front hall," I said. "I figured they must lead off the kitchen."

"Yes. This little cottage was built for an old retainer of the Comstocks'. They didn't waste any luxury on a servant."

"It's a funny name—Chêne Mow."

"There used to be a hawk coop here. That's what a mow is. It used to be called a mew. And *chêne* is French for oak. The royal stables at Charing Cross were built on the site of an old hawk mew. They went on calling it the mews, and the name spread to other stables. Nothing ever quite dies in England; it just becomes something else."

At the top of the stairs, a narrow hall was lit by a window at the near end. At the far end there was a door, with another door on either side halfway down the hall. Mollie led me toward the door at the end. "This is the master bedroom," she said, flinging open the little white-paneled door. "It runs along the whole width of the house at front. You'll want it for yourself, of course. It has a view of the road."

I felt a strange reluctance to follow her into the room, but shook the feeling away.

12

Two windows looked out on the road. The view from one of them was blocked by a gnarled old oak tree. At some time in the past the rough walls had been covered with blue wallpaper sprinkled with white blossoms. The uneven walls made the paper bumpy. A scattering of mismatched furniture lent the room a haphazard look. There was an old blue nylon flowered carpet on the floor.

In one corner of the room, though, I spotted a lovely antique lady's toilet table. It was apple green, with hand-painted pink flowers and white porcelain knobs. Its elegance was out of joint with the rest of the furnishings. Something in the room repelled me. I felt cold right through to my bones. Blue is a cold color, and that shaded window didn't help.

"Let's see the yellow room," I said.

Again I had that strange feeling that Mollie was smiling at me, though her lips didn't move. "Yes, let's see it," she said, and stood aside for me to go out first.

I opened the hall door on my left and stepped into a smaller but brighter room finished with wood paneling, painted a yellow that had darkened with time to a dull mustard shade. The furnishings were old, simple, but quite beautiful. A spool bed with a patchwork quilt, an oak dresser with a rounded front, a cheval glass in one corner, and one narrow window with a view of Chêne Bay towering above us.

"Yes, this is more like it!" I exclaimed.

13

"It's not nearly as big as the blue room. The last owner cut the end off this room to make the bathroom."

"It's big enough for me. Let's see the other bedroom."

We went into the last room. It was white-washed, with bunk beds and a matching varnished dresser, circa 1950. "The last people that stayed here had kids," Mollie said. "That was when the bunk beds were put in."

"I don't need two spare rooms. I'll sign the papers now," I said, and we went back downstairs to the sitting room to sign the rental contract and arrange the traveler's checks.

"Getting your groceries will be a bit of a problem when you don't have a car," Mollie pointed out.

"I'll rent one for the summer."

"That's no problem then. There's a car rental in Lyndhurst. Why don't you drive back with me, and you can pick up a few groceries?"

"That's a good idea. Thanks, Mollie. I'll get my luggage out of your car first."

She helped me bring it in, handed me the big brass key, and I locked the door with a proprietary feel. As we drove back into Lyndhurst, Mollie explained that the phone and hydro were included in the rent. Since the cottage was often rented for only a week or two at a time to tourists, this was the most convenient way to handle it.

She went with me into the car rental agency. After I had hired myself a white Morris Mini that was a replica of her own, but newer, she said, "How would you like a nice cuppa before you start your shopping?"

"A good idea. I haven't had lunch yet."

"The Pig and Whistle's your best bet," she advised. "You can get a nice ploughman's lunch and a pint at the pub for a couple of quid."

Mollie had the bread and cheese; I opted for a steak-and-kidney pie and a pint of ale, and felt I was seeing the real England. The windows of the pub were so old and thick and irregular, you could hardly see through them. A couple of elderly men were playing darts at the back of the room.

As Mollie sipped her second pint, she said in a tentative way, "What you said back at Chêne Mow, dear, about being interested in the psychic world..."

"I'd love to hear about it sometime."

I meant to listen with an open mind. A person's beliefs aren't, or shouldn't be, a subject for mockery. I had never taken that sort of thing seriously, but as Mollie seemed intelligent and was obviously sincere, I did her the courtesy of trying to understand.

"There is so much out there that people just ignore," she said, gesturing vaguely into the air with one shapely hand. "We—I belong to a group—try to tune into the wisdom of the universe, to read the messages that are all around us."

"What sort of messages? ESP, do you mean?"

"They might be messages from someone near and dear who is in trouble. You've heard of that sort of thing. A mother who knows instinctively when her child is in danger. Or it might be messages from the other side. That's a little more difficult. We have séances."

I thought of my father and felt a tremor of interest. "Anything else?" I asked.

"We're into healing with herbs, too, but mainly we work on developing our psychic powers. I often know what people are thinking. I knew you would take Chêne Mow, as soon as you saw it. I could feel a warm emanation from you, like the blast of a furnace. Why did you want the cottage, Belle?"

"I just liked the looks of it. Really."

"I see." She nodded, but I felt she didn't believe me. She continued talking about her group.

"It sounds interesting," I said. "Could I meet some of the other members?"

She smiled softly. "I sensed you were one of us. You have the power. You felt something in the blue bedroom, didn't you? I felt it myself, a definite presence. And you knew the other room was yellow, and about the knot garden. You're definitely psychic," she said firmly.

I shook my head. "I'd just been visiting

some of the stately homes. One of them had an Elizabethan knot garden. That's where that idea came from. I've never had a single extrasensory experience in my life, Mollie. I never know when people are going to call, or sense that someone is in trouble, or dead. You know, the sort of thing you read about."

"You have to work at it. I daresay Leonardo wouldn't have painted the *Mona Lisa* if he'd never practiced. Any talent has to be exercized to reach its full potential."

"I'm not really interested in becoming a psychic," I insisted. "What I actually had in mind was maybe incorporating it into a book I'm writing. Would you object to that?"

"Not in the least. I'll tell you what, come to the meeting with me tonight, and you can meet some of the others. We're having a séance at Thorndyke's farm. May Day was an important day in England's past—the fertility festival, you know. Something still lingers in the ether. It should be a good meeting. I'll pick you up, say, elevenish? The ceremony begins at midnight."

"I'll be ready."

We finished our lunch. Mollie went on to work, and I to buy my groceries and find my way home to Chêne Mow. I felt the whole thing was nonsense, but interesting nonsense. In my mind, it had about as much to do with reality as my daily horoscope, which I read faithfully but didn't believe. Still, it would be nice to receive some message from Dad.

Chapter Three

I stowed my groceries in the fridge and hanging cupboards and filled the teakettle. The location of Chêne Mow was somewhat inconvenient, the furnishings a confused jumble, the kitchen downright primitive, so it was hard to understand why I was so pleased with the place. I stood smiling at the plain deal table as I set out a cup and milk, planning to buy a couple of tablecloths to prettify the table. Maybe a blue and white checked gingham. I'd put wildflowers in a vase in the center of the table.

To pass the time until the kettle came to the boil, I wandered out into the garden. It was only an overgrown tangle of flowers, but I had never seen a garden that pleased me more. Pink and white peonies grew waist-high in front of a yew hedge that formed the barrier at the back of the cottage lot. Their heavy heads drooped under the weight of petals. Stalks of delphiniums were in bud but not in bloom. There were sweet peas and big daisies, dianthus, and a delicate, lacy vine, covering any bare patch of earth. Its delicate purple flowers suggested it might be lobelia. A fragrant perfume rose from the flowers, filling my lungs with the very essence of an English garden. I picked a bouquet and went around to the far side of the house.

There, tucked away against the yew hedge, was the Elizabethan knot garden. It was badly overgrown, but the original pattern was still discernible beneath the spreading ivy. The smoky gray of sage formed an X that crisscrossed the area. I recognized clumps of parsley and thyme, of basil and lovage, coriander and rue and mint. A bouquet garni of scents rose up as my ankles brushed the leaves. A bee droned lazily over the thyme. I picked enough parsley to flavor my dinner and add its peppery scent to the bouquet of flowers.

Beyond the hedge, I heard running water, and went to investigate. It was a stream, gliding softly over a floor of pebbles worn smooth by time. Farther up the hill toward Chêne Bay was its source. The stream had been dammed up to create a small lake. As the water flowed in, the lake overflowed to a lower level in a waterfall that lent novelty to the view. The water splashed in the sunlight, tossing crystal droplets into the air.

When I went back inside, the kettle was boiling. I made tea. My mind kept going back to the knot garden. I was pretty sure I had seen a picture of it, or one like it, in a book somewhere. It was probably a common pattern. It didn't mean anything that I knew how it would look before seeing it.

I put the dishes in the sink and took my bags upstairs to unpack. I took a peek into the blue bedroom. It wasn't my imagination that caused that chill. The room was at the north end of the house, where it got little sun. It was chilly, and the dark tree at the window didn't help. The coldness seemed to penetrate through to my bones. I turned and scuttled back to the more cheery yellow room.

After unpacking, I filled the tub in the tiny bathroom that had been severed from the yellow bedroom and had a leisurely soak. A shower would have been nice, but I could live without one for the summer. I wondered what a suitable outfit would be for attending a séance. Jeans and a jersey would be comfortable, but Mollie spoke of the séance with almost a religious fervor, and one does not wear jeans to church.

I chose a simple blue cotton dress. Forewarned of England's chilly evenings, I had brought a few sweaters and a woolen shawl with me. I'd take the shawl. When I was dressed, I went to the dresser to fix my hair and do my face. The loose, natural wave of my reddish-blond hair thrived in England's moist climate. All I had to do was brush back the bangs and let them tumble forward in waves. I inherited my late mother's blue eyes, pale complexion, and small, pointed chin. The only thing I inherited from my father was my tall, lean build. Seeing those blue eyes reminded me of Mom. She had died of a heart attack three years before. If she had still been alive, Dad's death wouldn't have hit me so hard. It was the double loss that did me in, and left me feeling betrayed.

When I was ready, I took up the shawl and went downstairs. It was six o'clock but still bright in the lengthening days of spring. I prowled around the house, discovering its secrets. The bookcase held me for an hour, poring over old copies of *Wuthering Heights* and Dickens and the romantic poets. At seven, I made an omelette and toast. After my snack, I began working on *Rebel Heart*.

I had brought a portable manual typewriter with me. Using it was like chopping wood after the luxury of the word processor at home, but it was better than writing by hand. I turned on the radio and had the Beatles for background accompaniment while I worked.

I enjoyed the solitude. Sometimes I felt Dad was right there, at my shoulder. There were several interruptions during the evening. At about nine o'clock I heard the first car pass, and saw the headlights moving up the road toward Chêne Bay. Businessmen, I assured myself, and returned to my novel. The car was soon followed by two or three more cars and a couple of trucks. Something to do with the video, I figured. At least there were no sounds of revelry from the big house.

Mollie arrived at ten after eleven. She was bareheaded and wore a loose white dress.

"I didn't know what to wear," I said. "I hope this is all right?"

"You didn't have to dress up, Belle. That's fine. I want to give you a little explanation of what you'll be seeing before we leave."

I made tea, and she gave me the general outline, most of which I was familiar with: the seating arrangement, the holding of hands, etc. When she had finished, we left. I took my notebook. This writer's constant companion was already stashed in my purse. We went in her car. At Chêne Bay, the video was being filmed outdoors. Banks of lights had been set up, casting an orange glow on the stone facade of the mansion. There was a small crowd—obviously something was going on.

Mollie drove for about three miles in the opposite direction from Lyndhurst until we came to one of those stretches of road where there were few houses. She turned in at a rutted laneway and bumped along through a tunnel of trees. I felt we were deep in the heart of some primitive country. It seemed a suitable habitat for wolves. Eventually we pulled free of the forest into a clearing. On the left, there was a dense thorn hedge, with gravestones behind it. The irregular white columns and crosses rearing into the darkness above lent a gothic air to the scene. On the right was a low, sprawling farmhouse. Mollie drove into the driveway and stopped. There were four or five other cars there before us.

"Henry Thorndyke is one of us," she said. "We usually meet at his place as it's centrally located for our group. Emily Millar will be conducting the séance. She's very good."

She tapped at the door and a middle-aged man who looked as if he might be a teacher or civil servant admitted us. Mollie introduced him as Henry Thorndyke. He showed us into an old-fashioned parlor and introduced me to the others. I expected Emily Millar to be a stately woman in black, with an air of affectation. She was a vague little lady with wispy gray hair, bags under her eyes, and a soft voice. She wore a pink blouse and tweed skirt.

"Mollie tells me you are to watch us tonight, Miss Savage. I'm sure you're very welcome." She turned to a younger woman who might have walked right out of a Dracula movie. She had jet black hair, worn long and straight. Her tall, lithe body was encased in a closely fitting black turtleneck sweater and slacks. She was not conventionally beautiful, but there was an air of distinction in her proudly held head.

"This is Sappho, our newest member," she said.

Of course, I wondered about the odd

name. Surely her parents hadn't named her after the famous poetess from Lesbos. Sappho shook my hand without saying anything. There were others, ten in all, ordinary-looking people. I met a schoolteacher and a secretary, a housewife and an accountant.

When everyone was assembled, Emily led the way into a low-ceilinged room across the hall. The only furnishings were a circular table and ten chairs surrounding it. Henry got me a chair from the parlor and set it at the edge of the room. Mollie had explained that they would all sit down in darkness and join hands on top of the table. Emily would act as the medium. Tonight she was trying to get in touch with her late husband. Her "guide" would be a spirit from the other world called Waldo. Emily would go into a trance. The communication would be by means of knocks on the table. Emily would ask questions. One knock meant the answer was no, two for yes.

It all seemed like something from a B movie. After the lights had been turned off and the group took their seats around the table and held hands, I sat peering through the shadows. The outline of their bent heads was visible by the light of a waning moon coming through glazed French doors at the far end of the room. It looked a little spooky, but not frightening. The hair on the back of my neck didn't lift when Emily began to utter a deep, humming

24

sound that showed she was going into her trance.

"Is that Waldo?" she asked.

As she spoke, a terrible skirling blast of wind battered beyond the windows. It was of near hurricane force. The doors rattled and blew open, letting in the howling wind, demonic in its fury. My hair blew in my eyes, and the notebook was torn from my fingers.

Until that moment, there had been no sense of a storm brewing. The sky had not darkened ominously. The air had not felt oppressive; there had been no little threatening gusts. Just the sudden, inexplicable onslaught of this howling wind. Treetops beyond the window bucketed, and branches bent under its fury. Twigs and small branches were torn from the trees and blew across the patio. A few dead leaves flew into the room. At the table, the group huddled together for protection, not uttering a sound. I thought they would have been shouting.

For a moment, I felt I was the cause of nature's wrath. My notebook seemed to be wrenched from my fingers by a superhuman presence. It was easy, at that moment, to believe that Emily had indeed called up some force from beyond the grave. I watched warily. Eventually the wind began to subside. As so often happens in ordinary life, it was a man who stepped forth to take charge.

"Best close the door, while we have the

chance," Henry said, and rose to do it. He had some trouble. The door seemed to be pushing against him, but eventually he got it shut.

"Perhaps we shouldn't have met on the eve of May Day," Emily said apologetically. "And with a waning moon, too. We'll forget it for tonight and try again another time."

Immediately the wind fell calm. The swaying treetops stilled, and stood unmoving once more.

Only a warm, gentle breeze remained. The door was closed now, but I could swear the breeze came from it. It seemed to envelop me, to curl itself around my arms and legs and body, like a lover, bringing an eerie sense of peace. The only sensation even vaguely similar to it occurred when I had once imbibed three margaritas in quick succession. I was not dizzy or intoxicated, but I felt a languorous golden ease seeping through me. I felt if I tried to walk, my legs would turn to rubber beneath me.

I was forced to the obvious conclusion: There was more to this psychic business than I had thought.

Chapter Four

We regrouped in Henry's comfortably shabby living room to discuss what the group were calling the "occurrence." He was a widower. A dreadful red wine was passed, and some cold-cut sandwiches. I wasn't hungry and I don't like red wine, but I found myself eating and drinking heartily, like the others. The wine, especially, was welcome to soothe the memory of what had happened in the parlor.

"It's plain as the tail on a dog that the rest of the area didn't get the storm," Henry said. "I took a look down the road. There's not a branch down except in my yard. That wind came from nowhere and went nowhere, except into the parlor. What do you think, Emily?"

We all looked for Emily's opinion, as she sat with her fingers massaging her temples. "I have a wretched headache," she said. "The vibrations were so very strong, I thought there must have been a manifestation. Did anyone see anything? There was definitely a spirit present."

After considerable discussion, the group agreed they had not seen anything, but several of them had felt a presence. We all drank a good deal of wine that night. Its rough edge was less noticeable after the third glass. Over the next hour, I had private conversations with as many of the psychics as I could. None of them had ever experienced anything like what we had seen that night.

"What I wonder," Emily said, "is what spirit came to us, and why. I had no feeling that it was my husband, nor was it Waldo. We must each light a candle when we get home, and see if it burns blue."

Sappho lifted her hair over her shoulder with a well-practiced gesture and said, "It could be Arabella. I've seen her in the meadow, from time to time."

"Who is Arabella?" I asked.

"She's a local ghost," Sappho explained. "She was murdered by a man called Vanejul a hundred and seventy-five years ago. She was the daughter at Chêne Bay. She walks the park, calling to Vanejul, asking him why he killed her, but she wasn't wailing when I saw her. She was just sobbing softly, and wringing her hands. Reminded me of Lady Macbeth."

"What meadow does she walk in?" I asked with a shiver. I wasn't in a mood to shrug off ghosts that night.

"The park at Chêne Bay, near the weir," she said. "You might see her, Belle, since you're stopping at Chêne Mow."

"You didn't tell me it was haunted, Mollie!" I said accusingly.

"Not Chêne Mow. Chêne Bay," Mollie said. "And it isn't the house. It's the parkland. Arabella haunts the weir, there where they've dammed up the water. You must have seen it."

"Oh, the dam. What does Arabella look like?"

"She's young and pretty. Fair-haired," Sappho said. "Of course, she wears old-fashioned clothes. A long dress and a bonnet. The bonnet was trailing down her back, held by its ribbons, when I saw her."

Emily, not to be outdone, said, "She's always wearing a flowered muslin gown when I see her—done in the empress style, you know, with a high waist. That would be the Regency period when she was murdered, somewhere around 1815."

"Around the time of Jane Austen," I mentioned.

"And Lord Byron and Beau Brummell," Emily added. "You can get a very good idea of how she would look from any Regency novel. You've heard of Georgette Heyer? I have her books, if you're interested."

"I've read a few of them. All about wicked guardians and runaway marriages and fortune hunters," I said.

"With fine lords and ladies"—Emily nodded. —"like Arabella. Our Arabella's lover was a lord. I always wonder why he killed her. Infidelity, I daresay. From what one reads, one would think he was the more likely to stray, for he had a reputation with the ladies. Their story would make a fine novel, only of course, the ending would be tragic, and readers of romance don't want that."

"The best romances end in tragedy," Sappho declared. "*Romeo and Juliet.* You've got the legend wrong, Emily, as usual. Arabella wasn't Vanejul's lover. He killed her because she didn't love him. She was engaged to another man. I've researched the story quite thoroughly. I'm thinking of writing a book about them."

A stab of anger pierced me. I put it

down to Sappho's rudeness to Emily, but as I listened to them argue, I realized that what I resented was Sappho's taking over of the legend. I didn't want her to write that particular book. I wanted to write that book myself. I was living on Arabella's estate, if not in her actual house. The idea intrigued me. *Rebel Heart* was stalled. I needed something completely different.

"I really should get writing the book," Sappho said.

Emily said sweetly, "And illustrate it with your little stick drawings, Sappho?"

"Those children's books are merely potboilers to pay the bills," Sappho retorted. "We weren't all born rich, Emily."

"Nor was I, dear. I married money. But then I was extraordinarily pretty."

"Long ago, when you were young, you mean," Sappho said.

It was after two o'clock when we parted. I was invited to call on some of the psychics, and invited them to call on me in turn. When we stepped out of Thorndyke's house, I thought of Ellie Duncan, and wondered if she was enjoying the pea souper that shrouded the countryside. The low-lying fog looked as if clouds had fallen from the sky and enveloped the earth in their airy mist. We passed only a few cars on the narrow road. Their approach was heralded by a sudden diffused glow in the fog.

"I gather that Sappho's a writer," I mentioned.

"She's best known for her illustrated children's books under the pen name Rosalie Lawson, but she also writes about the occult. She dresses dramatically in hopes that they'll interview her on the telly."

We were soon back at Chêne Mow. I invited Mollie in, but was glad when she refused. I was tired, and I had a lot to think about. I waved her off, then stood a moment, inhaling the fragrance of the English countryside—new-mown hay and sweet clover and blossoms. As my head was spinning from the wine, I decided to take a little fresh air before going indoors. Thinking about Arabella, I chose a moonlight stroll up toward the weir to see if I could catch a glimpse of her. I had no expectation of seeing a ghost. I thought the sightings might be due to some flowering bush that resembled a human shape in the mist. There were flowering shrubs in the park. The wailing voice could be caused by wind, or perhaps a cat or bird, or even by the viewer's having drunk too much.

I walked back to the roadway leading up the incline to Chêne Bay. The gravel crunching under my feet sounded loud in the stillness. Fog drifted in patches. The big house loomed high on the hill above the mist, its cupola etched in black against the silver sky. There were a few lighted windows downstairs, but no sign of the video makers outdoors. A faint echo of music reached my ears as I drew closer to the house. The rippling sound of the waterfall echoed in the distance.

I enjoyed the fog and the quiet music. It wasn't the raucous noise of Roarshock, but a waltz. Perhaps the businessmen preferred that more peaceful music. It didn't occur to me to be afraid, probably because of all the wine I had drunk. I soon caught a glimpse of sparkling water to the right. The long grass wrapped itself around my ankles as I left the road and hurried forward, scanning the park for Arabella, or a bush of vaguely human shape.

I was soon at the waterfall. It was no Niagara, but a sedate man-made affair, the barrier below the water as straight as a ruler. The water did not gush, but flowed. Still, there is always some enchantment in moving water, and I stood gazing at it, then to the dammed water above it. I wondered how deep the water was. At night it looked black, fathomless. Was it deep enough to drown? Was this where Arabella had met her fate? The reports of people having seen her here suggested it.

If so, I was definitely not psychic, for to me the spot seemed enchanted, in spite of the dark water and shadows all around. The shadows were not frightening, but friendly. It was a romantic spot for a lovers' tryst.

The fog shifted, and suddenly the water disappeared from view. I was in the middle of an earthbound cloud. I felt one fleeting instant of panic, then a strange calm came over me, like the eerie peace I had felt when the wind calmed at the séance. The moist air had that same gentle warmth, as it hugged me close in its embrace. The fog shifted again, and through a lingering veil of mist, a human form appeared. The outline firmed to reveal a young man.

He was tall and dark-haired and wickedly handsome. The air caught in my lungs at the sight of him, appearing so unexpectedly. There was a hint of the rake in his sparkling, black-diamond eyes, which studied me with the gaze of a connoisseur studying a painting. That look spoke of admiration bestowed by one who was qualified to judge. I felt that from his infinite knowledge of women, he was awarding me the golden apple. His full lips lifted in pleasure, or excitement. His skin looked swarthy, though it was difficult to be certain at night. I could see that his features were regular, with a strongly arched nose and a firm chin. Just the sort of hero you see on dust covers.

Adding to this fictional effect was his outfit, for he was dressed in some sort of historical costume, with a white cravat rising high above the lapels of a jacket not seen since the nineteenth century. The intricate folds of his immaculate cravat contrasted dramatically with his dark skin. His trousers were roughly the cut of riding jodhpurs; high black leather boots rose to just below his knees.

My first thought was that I was having

a hallucination; then the absurd idea took hold that I was seeing a ghost. Finally the truth dawned on me. He was an actor in the video that was being shot at Chêne Bay. Looking like a hero, and looking at a woman as if he loved her, were his stock in trade. That carefully barbered hair was probably held in place by buckets of hairspray. Perhaps his long lashes were even cosmetically enhanced. While we stared at each other without saying a word, his first spontaneous show of admiration dwindled to a scowl.

"I'm trespassing," I said. My voice was breathless. He didn't answer, but just continued to glare. "I've rented Chêne Mow," I said, gesturing toward it. "My name is—"

"I know who you are, and why you're here," he said, with an impatient gesture of his elegant hands.

"Are you in the video?" I asked.

His curt snort was full of contempt. "Do I look like one of those yahoos, with ladies' jewelry rattling about them like a tinker man?"

"No, you don't. Is there a masquerade party going on? That looks like a costume from the last century."

He glanced down at his jacket. "It was a come-as-you-are party," he said, with a cynical smile.

Was he saying he always dressed up like this? England is famous for its eccentrics. It is a part of its allure for Americans.

We are infatuated by a people who really don't care what others think of them. The man looked at me so impatiently, I thought I should leave, before I was hinted away.

"Well, it's late. I should be going."

"What is time to *us*?" he asked softly. That "us" had a burr of intimacy to it, as if we two were set apart in some manner from the rest of mankind. He put his hand on my wrist, with a touch so light, I hardly felt it. His fingers were long and graceful. On the small finger of his left hand he wore an engraved emerald ring. "Come, let us go," he said, looking up toward Chêne Bay. The waltz music sounded louder. "They are playing Gardel's *Dansomanie*. Remember it? We shall have a waltz, just you and I."

There must have been a madness in the air, because I felt a strong inclination to go with him, but common sense won out. To go to a punk rocker's house alone with a strange man at this hour was asking for trouble. This matinee idol probably expected me to fall into his bed. Besides, I was beginning to wonder if he hadn't been indulging in some illegal substance. There was a distracted air about him.

"It's much too late! I must go," I said, sliding easily from his grasp.

"Still a coward, Belle?" he taunted.

"I am not a coward! And how did you know my name?" He didn't deign to answer my question. In fact, he looked surprised that I had asked it. Perhaps he had learned it from the owner of Chêne Bay. Mollie might have notified Ivan the Terrible, although it seemed unlikely Ivan would have bothered to discuss me with his guests. "Who told you my name?"

He smiled tolerantly. "What else would such a *belle fille* be called?"

"I'm twenty-six years old, not exactly a girl."

"A bit long in the tooth to be sure," he laughed, "but you will always be sweet sixteen to *me*, Belle. Why did you come here tonight?"

"I was looking for Arabella."

"Surely that is redundant! I hoped you were looking for me."

"How should I know you'd be here?"

He adopted a playful manner, as though we were sharing a joke. "Oh, I am often in the neighborhood, also looking for Arabella."

"Who are you, a ghost hunter?"

He stared as if I had struck him. "Good God, don't you recognize me?"

I studied his handsome face in the mist. There was something oddly familiar about it, but it was only an inkling, a tantalizing echo from the past. Was he a well-known movie star? Some of the videos hired actors for guest shots. "I'm afraid I don't."

He struck his breast in a melodramatic gesture. "Wounded to the quick!" Then he laughed again. "Liar!" he taunted softly, as his arms reached confidently for me.

"Perhaps if you gave me a clue..."

A reckless light gleamed in his wicked eyes. "That might be best," he agreed, and swept me into his arms.

It was at that moment I realized I was hallucinating. His arms were not flesh-and-blood arms. There was no flesh, no sinew, no muscle to them; they were only the comfortable warmth I had been feeling earlier. His lips pressed mine, but with a phantom kiss that generated a longing they could not satisfy, almost as though he were an image projected on a screen. The very archetype of the romantic lover held me in his arms, the handsome stranger women have been dreaming of for centuries. He carried on his shoulders the mystery of past ages when ladies rode pedestals, and gentlemen performed heroic deeds to win their favors. He was ideal, infinite man. He was the hero of *Rebel Heart*! I had found him! He had sprung from the depths of my subconscious, complete in every detail, lacking only physical substance.

These ideas reeled in my head while I was held in thrall by the magical warmth of his phantom embrace. As the kiss deepened, the hunger grew inexorably, and I learned the meaning of the word *frustration*. It was the thirsting man's mirage of water in the desert, the starving man's dream of food that vanished on its way to his lips, the philosopher's hunger for the truth.

"Who are you?" I gasped, drawing back from him.

His hand, fading now to an insubstantial shadow, lifted my fingers to his lips for a ghost kiss, as fleeting as the brush of a moth's wing. "Ah, Belle," he said, with such a sad look that my heart was wrenched.

Then he was gone, taking the warmth with him, and I was left alone in the fog by the weir, bewildered and ineffably saddened.

Chapter Five

I have to this day no memory of returning from the weir that night. I awoke the next morning in the blue room that I had spurned the day before as being too cold. My objection seemed foolish now. Perhaps the room had been a little chilly, but in the light of a new spring morning, it was fine.

I lay in bed awhile, nursing a woolen tongue and a hangover from the cheap red wine, thinking about the séance, and the "occurrence" that had disrupted it. I knew I must have been quite drunk when I got home, because I couldn't remember coming upstairs, and if I had been sober, I would have slept in the yellow room. I remembered a strangely vivid dream about meeting a handsome, strange man in the park by the weir. My dreams usually fade as soon as I get up, but that one stayed with me while I washed and dressed in jeans and a fleecy shirt.

His image was as sharp as if he were still

with me while I brewed coffee in an antique metal pot with a little glass bubble in the lid. I toasted whole wheat bread and peeled a perfect pear.

I made some tentative plans for my day while I ate. In the morning I'd work on the hero of *Rebel Heart*, get the stranger from the weir down on paper while the image was still fresh. And in the afternoon I'd try to get hold of Mollie to clarify a few details of the séance, in case I ever wrote about it. I wanted to speak to some of the others as well. One viewpoint wasn't enough. Emily was the oldest, and most experienced. She'd invited me to call on her.

I put my portable typewriter on the deal table in the kitchen as it provided the closest thing to a desk. It was hard to concentrate with sunlight streaming in at the window and that untended garden begging for attention. The image of the dream stranger was still so sharp in my mind that it seemed redundant to write a description of him. The word *redundant* sounded a familiar echo. *Surely that is redundant!* I could almost hear someone say it—a man's voice. I shook the thought away and continued my work.

My editor, Anne Morrissey, had begun hounding me about *Rebel Heart*, but what I really wanted to write was Arabella's story. It intrigued me, which is odd, for it was not my special period, and there was really not much to it. Just the tale of a young woman who had jilted her lover, or refused to become the man's lover, or something, and been murdered by him. Perhaps it tweaked my interest because of the unrequited romance and the ghost.

It would still be a historical novel, but set in the early nineteenth century instead of the seventeenth. The Regency period, Emily had called it. I was familiar with Byron and Austen, but I'd have to buy or beg more books from the period to get the zeitgeist and terminology. Anachronisms were anathema to readers of historical fiction.

My attention strayed back to the dream stranger. He needed a name, something gallant and dashing, yet with a touch of class. I was just going to the fridge to scrounge for lunch when there was a tap at the door. I opened it to see Mollie. Her gleaming eyes told me she was up to some new mischief.

"It's been confirmed," she announced, stepping in. She wore another of her wildly flowered balloons, with the same pink spike-heeled shoes. "We did raise a spirit last night. I've been around to Emily's place. Her candle burned blue, too. Did I tell you mine did?"

"No. Does that mean there's a spirit abroad?"

"Of course!"

I led her to the kitchen and poured her a cup of coffee. She ladled in an unconscionable quantity of sugar and cream, stirred distractedly, and continued chattering.

"I lit my candle the minute I got home.

There was definitely a presence. I felt it even before the candle burned blue." She leaned toward me, green eyes sparkling. "It was in a wicked temper, Belle. It tossed the candle right onto the floor and darn near burned the house down. I was worried about you, here so close to the meadow where she roams."

"You think it was Arabella?"

"That's what Emily thinks. Of course, it was Arabella who was murdered, and disturbed spirits do walk. But so do evil spirits. I'm quite sure this one was a man."

"Why do you think that? Does the candle burn differently for a man?"

"No, but I sense a woman's presence in the head and heart. I feel a male in the loins. The sensation was so strong that I know my spirit was a rake. You didn't experience anything, you being so close to Chêne Bay?"

"No, I didn't." She looked disappointed. I said, "But I had a really weird dream about a man. He was dressed in the costume of the Regency period. I suppose all that talk at Thorndyke's place filled my head with ideas."

She asked eagerly, "What did he look like?"

I closed my eyes, and the image of him returned, clear and vivid. "He was tall, with black hair, handsome. He asked me what I was doing at the weir, and when I said I was looking for Arabella, he said he was looking for her, too."

"That sounds like Vanejul."

"The man who killed her?"

"That's right. He was her lover, whatever Sappho may say. She always has to be different. Mind you, a lover in those days might mean no more than a boyfriend. He was a handsome rascal, to go by the pictures. Or it could have been the other man in her life, the one she was engaged to."

"As I said, it was only a dream, but a vivid one."

"You're sure it was a dream?" she asked archly. "Are you sure you're not fooling yourself? A state of denial is quite common on a person's first encounter with the spirit world. Same as when you catch a fatal disease."

"I'm sure. How did Vanejul murder Arabella?"

"According to the legend, he drowned her in the weir when she jilted him. They never found her body, but someone saw him do it. The books say Arabella got an offer from some man she liked better and gave Vanejul the boot. I don't know how she had the heart to do it, for he was fascinating. Perhaps it was just a dream you had. Vanejul would have no reason to come back. He wasn't murdered."

"What did happen to him?"

"He died of a fever in Greece years after Arabella's death. His body was sent home. It's buried at Oldstead Abbey, about ten miles north of here. The

Raventhorpes still live there. His real name was Baron Raventhorpe. Vanejul was his nom de plume. He wrote poetry."

"Did he ever go to trial?"

"Devil a bit of it. He drowned poor Arabella, then ran off and caught the first ship out of England before they could find him. According to the writings that came out after his death, he went straight to the bad, whoring around Europe with anything in a skirt. Mind you, he left some wonderful poetry for posterity."

"I've heard of Vanejul. He wasn't one of the major romantic poets, though. Not like Wordsworth or Byron. I read a few of his poems when I was in college. They were a little cynical for my taste, although his first few love poems were tender and romantic."

"That'd be the stuff he wrote before he went to Greece. There are all kinds of books about him in the local shops, if you're interested. This is Vanejul territory."

"Vanejul—that's an anagram for Juvenal, isn't it? Some famous Englishman used that pen name for a column he used to write in the journals, to hide his identity. Sydney Smith, they think it was."

"I don't know about that, but around here everybody knows Raventhorpe as Vanejul."

"I wonder why he didn't publish under his own name."

"He was wanted for murder, that's why. Not that he would have been easy to find

43

in a foreign country in those days, I suppose, before they had telephones and fax machines. There was a big war going on as well, the Napoleonic war. Vanejul's real identity wasn't discovered until after he was dead."

"I'll drive into Lyndhurst this afternoon and see if I can find some books. Actually I'm more interested in Arabella."

Mollie shook her head. "You won't find much on her. There's a chapter on her in a book about ghosts in famous English mansions, but she never did anything to merit a book of her own. Not many women did in the old days, unless they were queens or courtesans. And of course, she died young."

Tracking down the research was beginning to seem a formidable task.

"Why are you so interested, if you don't mind my asking?" Mollie said. "Are you thinking of writing about her?"

"Maybe, if I could find enough material."

"Sappho talks about doing a book, but I think it's Vanejul she's more interested in. She's all talk, that one. You might find enough for an article on Arabella's legend. She's mostly just a footnote in books on Vanejul. I'll tell you who might be able to help you, is Emily Millar. She's some kin to the Throckleys. You can bet she'll never help Sappho."

What Emily had would only be hearsay, but better than nothing. "Emily asked me to call. Where does she live?"

"In that big stone mansion just on the edge of Lyndhurst. Emily's loaded. The only reason Matt Millar ever married her was because of her noble connections. They cut quite a swath in society when he was alive, and she was younger. She's related to the Raventhorpes and a few other noble houses as well. There's a lot of inbreeding in the aristocracy."

"Was Arabella from a noble family?"

"Maybe related to the nobility, but she didn't have a title. You can tell by Chêne Bay the Comstocks were very rich, and wealth usually means power."

We finished our coffee, and Mollie rose. "I have to show a cottage this afternoon. Another retired civil servant wants to come to the New Forest to paint. If all the amateur paintings of the New Forest were put end to end, they'd reach China. And China is welcome to them. I'll be in touch."

I accompanied her to the door. Just before leaving, she grabbed my hand and said, "You'll let me know if anything happens. You know—about the occurrence. There's definitely a spirit out there." She waved and hobbled out to her car.

I didn't think anything supernatural would occur. I was halfway to convincing myself that nothing out of the ordinary had happened last night. The strange ritual had heightened my imagination, but all I had actually seen was a violent, short burst of wind and a door blowing open. Geography affected the wind currents. High buildings in cities, for instance, caused terrific winds. Maybe Thorndyke's farm was located in a wind belt. No doubt there was a rational explanation.

My immediate concern was lunch. I collected some herbs from the knot garden, prepared a herb omelette, ate it while reading over my morning's work, and set off for Lyndhurst.

I didn't feel confident in the English car yet, driving on the wrong side of the road. I encountered another goose who assumed a fowl took precedence over a car, and had to give her the right of way. The short drive left me nervous.

Chapter Six

Once I reached Lyndhurst, I set aside my cares, and for the next hour I forgot all about driving and ghosts. I just prowled the picturesque little town like any tourist, examining the crafts for sale and the amateur paintings of the New Forest, picking up postcards to send home, and buying the few dozen items required for temporary residence in a hired house. There was no blue checked tablecloth to be had; I bought a plain blue one, and found a pretty milk glass vase in an antique store.

The variety of English accents and the peculiar idioms were a novelty. I wasn't used to hearing myself called "luv" by total strangers. I visited an old Norman stone church, perhaps the one Arabella attended. For some reason, the church reminded me of her, and I went in search of books. A corner bookstore with a bay window jutting right into the street held a large selection of glossy historical books on the region, probably for the tourist trade. The works of Sappho in her Rosalie Lawson guise were also lavishly represented. The protagonists of her books were a red rooster called Shanty Clear and a white cat called Blanche. I thumbed through one. It was in rhyme, and rather clever, although the drawings were not very good.

What I could not find was anything on either Arabella or Vanejul. The clerk suggested the library, but I mark the books I use for research—turn down pages and underline passages, scribble notes on the flyleaf to save time when referring back to something. I couldn't deface a library book. I went back into the street, disappointed.

One of these days I'd get to London, where I was sure to find what I wanted. I headed back to my car. I don't know what made me go into the tobacco shop, because I don't smoke, and the literature purveyed there held lurid covers of scantily clad women bound in chains. The newspaper headlines screamed of a woman who had given birth to a three-year-old child. Normally I avoid such places, but something urged me to go in.

Toward the rear of the shop, a section

of the wall about six feet square held an assortment of pornographic magazines and paperbacks. Men with lust-glazed eyes thumbed the books. I was about to leave when something—I can only call it an intuition—held me. I peered quickly along the racks, and there, just at the far end, the word *Vanejul* hit me in the eye. It was a paperback, and the cover illustration showed him in an outfit like Count Dracula's, with a flowing cape lined in crimson. In his arms he held a sodden young woman, presumably Arabella. Long blond hair streamed over her shoulders. A mound of bosoms that put Dolly Parton to shame rose from her low-cut scarlet bodice. A pair of fulsome lips pouted enticingly, even in death. He stood at the edge of a pool of dark, dank water. A stark black tree soared behind him, with the inevitable pale moon above. It was a shameless depiction of Freudian symbolism.

I snatched the book up, paid the clerk, and ran from the shop, glad that no one would recognize me. I drove home at once, reveling in the serendipity of having gone into that sleazy shop. What had possessed me to do it? At home, I put away my purchases, brewed a pot of tea, and settled in at the kitchen table to examine my find. Despite the lurid cover, it was a perfectly respectable work. The hardcover publisher from whom the paperback rights came confirmed it. The introduction assured me it was the definitive work on

Vanejul, written by Professor Thumm, from Oxford University. As the original publication date was 1949, I assumed Professor Thumm was either dead or too old to give me an interview.

It was a chunky anthology nearly two inches thick containing the poetry, explanatory notes, letters and diaries, and a longish biography of Vanejul. Such a book is hard to read since it doesn't like to stay open. I mercilessly forced it open, breaking the spine in the process, and began to read. First a few selections from the early poetry. As I recalled, the early poems were tenderly romantic, in the vein of Keats or Shelley. A clever turn of phrase here, a vivid image there, saved them from being maudlin.

I flipped on to the later satirical verses. The cleverness was greatly increased, but a cynicism had crept in. They were the outpourings of a hardened misogynist. The hero was the author, Vanejul. After reading three longish poems, I had discerned the theme. An innocent man fell in love with a worldly woman, often married, who betrayed him. He took his revenge on her, usually by ruining her reputation. The revenges were arranged in diabolically clever ways, with much detail. I felt Vanejul thoroughly enjoyed plotting out these revenges. In one poem Laura was lured to a country inn to meet her new lover, after jilting Vanejul. Vanejul arranged for the husband to meet his lover at the same inn at

49

the same time, and catch his wife in flagrante delicto.

In another poem, the lady was lured to a deserted spot deep in the country, supposedly to retrieve her billets-doux from Vanejul, who had been jilted once again. She rather foolishly sent her coachman off, expecting Vanejul to carry her home. He never came, stranding her there. To heighten the poor lady's chagrin, she was missing her own birthday party. The sort of thing Byron might have written in *Don Juan*.

Vanejul's poems had been naughty in their day, no doubt, but reeked of mothballs in today's lenient sexual climate. They were flippantly sophisticated and done with tongue-in-cheek humor, but nasty and mean-spirited at the core. Definitely the work of a misogynist. It was all rather childish. The revenges were related with hand-rubbing glee, as if Vanejul gloried in hurting and humiliating women. Yet despite his invariably being jilted, he kept on chasing them, like a man obsessed. After fifty pages, I wanted to shake him, to tell him to grow up and stop wasting his talent. I tossed the book aside.

I had treated myself to a steak for dinner, and bought a couple of bottles of wine. I took my dinner to the living room so the television could keep me company while I ate. It was the usual litany of bad news—riots, wars, murders, with more talk of the European Common Market than we got at home. My wandering mind came to riveted attention when I heard the name Lord Raventhorpe. I darted forward and turned up the volume.

"Lord Raventhorpe remains in critical condition in hospital in Stratford-upon-Avon following a motorcycle accident yesterday afternoon. He collided with a lorry. He underwent emergency surgery late last night. The police are investigating. And on the political front, the prime minister is in Belgium today..."

I turned the volume down and went back to my steak. That I had been reading Vanejul shortly before the announcement was just one of those strange coincidences that occur from time to time. Synchronicity, Carl Jung would call it. To add to the coincidence, I must have been near the scene of the accident when it happened. I had been on the road from Stratford yesterday afternoon. I had even seen a motorcycle driving erratically. I remembered that black helmet and masked face appearing at the bus window; it had seemed to be looking right at me. Drops of ice water trickled down my spine. That man couldn't be Baron Raventhorpe! That would be too much coincidence. No, of course it wasn't. There were hundreds of motorcycles on the roads. But it was strange that Raventhorpe had been driving one. I would have thought a baron would drive a Rolls, or a Jaguar.

When the telephone shrilled in the

kitchen, I froze, and was half-afraid to answer it. What did I think? That it was Baron Raventhorpe calling from his sickbed? Get real! I jumped up and lifted the receiver.

"Belle, it's me, Mollie. I was just listening to the telly. Did you hear about Lord Raventhorpe?"

"Yes, I just heard it. Quite a coincidence."

"I wonder if it has anything to do with *the occurrence*," she said, giving the words italics.

"What do you mean?"

"I don't know—it's just odd, his having an emergency operation late last night, maybe about the time of the occurrence. He must have taken a sudden turn for the worse, or why did they take so long to operate? What I'm saying is, he may have died for a bit, or been on the edge of death, with his spirit escaping and finding its way to the séance."

I just shook my head. Why would the present Raventhorpe fly to Henry Thorndyke's meadow? "If that's the case, you can stop worrying, Mollie. He's still alive, presumably with his spirit back in his body."

"Yes," she said. "That's true. You haven't had any odd occurrences at Chêne Mow?"

"No, everything's normal. Did the artist buy the cottage?"

"He's made an offer the seller will never accept, and he wants the furniture thrown in to boot. But about Raventhorpe..."

I had hoped we were finished with that idea. "I got a copy of a book about him," I said. "I've been reading it this afternoon."

"Oh yes. But what I meant was about his spirit. It could have been him that I conjured up last night. You remember I told you it was a male spirit."

"Yes, you mentioned feeling him in your loins," I said, glad she couldn't see the smirk on my face. "Is the present Lord Raventhorpe a famous rake as well, then?"

"As a matter of fact, he is inclined that way, but I was confusing him with his relative, Vanejul. That would mean that the nineteenth-century Raventhorpe had been reincarnated in the present one, and that would be pretty unusual. There can't be anything to it. Frank's candle burned blue, too, by the way."

"That spirit certainly got around!"

"They're not like real people. They can diffuse their ether, and be more than one place at once. Anyway, we've decided to have an informal meeting at Emily's place tonight. Emily, me, and Henry Thorndyke. Would you like to come?"

"Some other time, Mollie. I'm busy tonight," I said.

I was finding that a little of the occult went a long way with me. I'd go to the pub and try to meet some people my own age.

"So you've met a man. Is he handsome?" she asked, and laughed. I gave a small answering laugh that seemed to satisfy her. "I'll let you know what happens. Have fun."

"You, too, Mollie."

I hung up and just shook my head. What remained of my dinner had grown cold, but I finished it anyway as I didn't want to waste an expensive steak.

Twilight was drawing in, and I went out for a walk before it grew dark. Mollie hadn't mentioned whether I was allowed to walk in the park, but I knew the English were more broad-minded in that respect than we were at home. It seemed odd to me that you could pay and tour many of the mansions here as well, even ones with people still living in them. I walked up toward the weir, with the shadows growing long on the grass. Birds soared overhead, saying good-bye to a beautiful spring day. The sky was a pastel abstract of peach and lemon slashes, fading to violet near the eastern horizon. Falling petals from the flowering bushes swirled to the ground like perfumed snowflakes.

I remembered my dream, and the handsome man who had kissed me. He had said he was looking for Arabella. Perhaps he was my mind's interpretation of the man Arabella was going to marry, the one for whom she had jilted Vanejul. No one had mentioned his name, but if that was who he was, I felt Arabella had made a wise choice to ditch Vanejul. A sixteen-year-old maiden would be tender fodder for his cannon.

As I stood, looking at the water and thinking, a fire-engine red Alfa Romeo zoomed down from Chêne Bay. A man with purple spiked hair honked the horn, leaned out, leered, and shouted a friendly greeting. Ivan didn't stop, and he didn't seem to mind that I was trespassing. There was no sign of the people making the video. Perhaps they had finished. I meant to find out what group it was, so I could watch for the video when it came out. I was beginning to feel proprietary about the neighborhood.

When I returned to Chêne Mow, I felt restless, alone in the house. All those empty rooms seemed to weigh on my mind, making me uneasy. It was too early to go to the pub. I phoned Emily to ask her if I could call tomorrow, and also to hear a human voice. She invited me to tea at three. I envisaged something elegant: thin cucumber sandwiches, and tea served in translucent china cups. It made me realize how rustic my cottage was. I cleared the table and put on the blue cloth, gathered a few flowers for the milk glass vase and put them in the center. The patter of rain against the windows was enough to keep me from going into town.

I poured a glass of sauternes and took Vanejul to the sofa for a long read of the biographical part of the book. Arabella was scarcely mentioned. Professor Thumm wrote that Vanejul had been in love with her. He didn't say whether she had loved him. He suggested that an ungovernable streak in the Raventhorpe blood was the reason for Arabella's refusal to marry him. In his youth, Vanejul's father had apparently killed a man in a duel over a lady—not the lady he eventually married.

The professor hypothesized that when Arabella had become betrothed to another man, Raventhorpe, in a fit of passion, had killed her. There wasn't much solid fact. He wrote about the other man in her life; he was William Throckley, son of Sir Giles Throckley, Arabella's cousin and guardian. That would make William and Arabella cousins as well, but marriages were often arranged within the family in those days, especially when fortunes were involved. Both Throckleys, father and son, were dull, sterling characters. The son went on to play a small role in national politics.

There seemed no doubt whatsoever that Vanejul had led a life of licentiousness and vice in Greece and Italy. Actually he spent more time in Italy than Greece, and it was odd his later career was referred to as his Grecian phase. But he died fighting for Greece's independence, and thus his name became associated with it.

To soften the cynicism of the man, there was also a wide streak of generosity in him. He gave liberally to the poor, and apparently supported several struggling writers and painters outright. He even paid the monumental debts of one of his mistress's husbands. Charitable indeed! He was involved in a series of scrapes with influential Italians. The journal excerpts chronicling his darts about from Ravenna to Venice to Naples, with assorted officials, *carbonari*, angry fathers, husbands, brothers, and mistresses dogging his trail, were amusing. That he always had friends to aid and abet him suggested he possessed a certain charm. His prose was written in an eminently readable style. I could almost feel I was there, watching his wicked doings. I preferred his prose to his poetry. Vanejul was a novelist manqué.

It was impossible for a woman to admire him, and equally impossible not to feel a grudging interest. He was the sort of rake we would all like to think we alone have the power to reform. If only I had known him! It was easy enough to see why men through the years liked him. He led the scandalous life of a wealthy vagabond, doing just as he pleased, always surrounded by eager women. And there was the generosity, the humor, and eventually the heroic death to enshrine him in a dubious sort of respectability. Altogether a fascinating character, but one felt somehow sullied to read of his exploits.

When I glanced at my watch, I was astonished to see it was one-thirty. I had a glass of milk and went straight up to bed.

Chapter Seven

I awoke in the morning in the blue room with a deep ache in my heart, and some fast-fading fragments of a dream hovering at the edge of memory. I had dreamed again of him, that illusory ephemera, my phantom lover. He had come to me in the night. No spoken words remained in memory, but only a sense of anger so diffuse, I could not say whether it was he or I who had been angry. If I closed my eyes, I could almost remember his dark eyes flashing, his hot lips uttering accusations, which I was quick to refute. I had no idea what we had been debating, or who had won. I felt a great yawning emptiness within, and tried to convince myself it was only hunger.

But the empty feeling continued after I had taken breakfast. Writing was impossible in such a restless state of mind, so I went to the garden to begin the weeding. At that primitive occupation I found peace. The warm sun beat on my shoulders as I rooted out the weeds, tossing them onto the compost pile. The flowers bloomed well enough along the border, but at the very heart of the garden, strangled flower stalks had grown pale and weak from lack of nourishment. Buds had withered. Those that had opened were stunted, but the stems could not support even these small blooms without the undergrowth of weeds. I felt, somehow, that the garden was whispering its ancient wisdom to me. People, too, must clear the underbrush out of their lives from time to time.

An hour was enough to clear my head. I went indoors and wrote until noon. The interval until three, I spent with Vanejul, finishing the cynical poems and rereading bits of the biography and journals. Expecting to find them faintly repulsive, I was surprised to discover my heart had softened. A man was not born a misogynist. Vanejul had obviously been hurt by someone. Perhaps he had truly been in love with Arabella.... What sort of woman was she? Had she been a Laura in training, with already the seeds of coquetry sprouting? I refer to the Laura of Vanejul's poem, not Petrarch's Laura.

I had read the book to learn what I could about Arabella, but I found my interest, and even my sympathy, begin to change direction. I had to pull myself up sharply. Whatever she had done, he had no right to kill her. This Vanejul was an insidious character. If letters on a page could so easily warp judgment, what must the man have been like in person? I was very curious to see his picture, and Arabella's, too. The paperback had no illustrations. I would stop at the library after taking tea with Emily. Surely the Lyndhurst library must have books on these local celebrities.

As Emily Millar inhabited one of the finest houses in town and was connected to noble families, I thought a dress might be called for. I chose a white one with green flowers, fluffed out my hair, did my face, and was off.

Driving on the left side of the road still seemed wrong, but I was getting the hang of it now. I reached Emily's house without incident. No butler met me at the door, as I had been hoping. Emily answered it herself, wearing plaid slacks and a wilted heather sweater that she called a jumper.

"Don't you look nice, Belle!" she said. "I've put on this old jumper and slacks. Come in. I've got the kettle on."

No servants were in evidence as she led me into a grand house that would require two or three to keep it in shape. And it was in good shape. The gray marble-floored hallway gleamed. A curved stairway to the left of the entrance also had marble steps and an ornate cast-iron railing. I peered into the main saloon at Persian carpets, long windows with gold satin, pelmeted draperies, what looked like an Adam fireplace, and good antique furnishings.

"We'll take tea in the morning parlor," she said. "I had a small fire laid to take the chill off."

I followed her down the hallway to a cozy little parlor that looked out on a weedless garden. The shabbily comfortable room was done in what the decorating magazines call

"English country" style, but more dilapidated. The carpet was quite bare, and the sofa sagged, but there were masses of fresh flowers on tables and an interesting grouping of nature prints on the wall.

"Have a seat, Belle. We'll sit by the fire. Millie will bring our tea presently. She's my char; she comes in daily. Live-in servants are impossible to get nowadays. It's like looking for the Holy Grail to find good servants."

Millie duly appeared, bearing a fine old silver tea service and sturdy mugs from Woolworth's. There were no cucumber sandwiches. She served Fig Newtons, which I dislike. Millie was a teenager with a blond ponytail and a sullen expression. When she clattered the tea tray onto the table, I understood why Emily did not use fine china. Emily poured and handed me a cup.

"I'm glad you dropped by, Belle," she said, with a question in her eyes. She was wondering why I had.

"How did the meeting go last night?" I asked. "Mollie mentioned you and Henry and she were meeting."

"It was only a partial success. We all agreed a spirit was trying to get through, but he could not make it. Very odd."

"The reason I came, Emily, I want to write something on the Arabella legend. Mollie mentioned you are some connection to her. I thought you might have some family papers."

"Oh no, dear. They were kept at Chêne Bay. Gord Throckley handed the whole thing over to some university. Oxford, I suppose it would be. He attended Oxford. You might find something at the Bodleian. But I can tell you there was nothing of Arabella's in it. It was just boring old family documents about buying land and marriage records and that sort of thing."

"I hoped there might be some letters from Raventhorpe, or perhaps a diary."

"A poet like Vanejul must have written her marvelous love letters," she sighed. "But I suppose when she jilted him, she gave them back to him. They did that in those days. The Vanejul papers are at Oldstead Abbey. They made them available to Dr. Thumm. If it is a serious, critical work you are doing, they might let you see them. They don't encourage scandalmongers. You would have to send your résumé and a letter from your editor."

I had no contract with any editor to write about Arabella. I doubted if my list of credits from half a dozen minor American magazines and one historical paperback novel would cut any ice with the Raventhorpes.

"Of course, you couldn't pester them at this time," she continued. "You heard about young Adam's accident?"

"Lord Raventhorpe? Yes, I heard it on the TV last night."

"Lily, Lady Raventhorpe, is in London.

The father is dead. It's touch and go with Adam. I must send Lily a note."

"Does Adam look anything like Vanejul?"

"I see some family resemblance around the eyes and hairline, but he is not as dashing as Vanejul."

She poured another cup of tea, nibbled a Fig Newton, then spoke. "Mollie feels you are psychic," she said, peering at me from the corner of her eyes. "You seemed to have some knowledge of Chêne Mow before seeing it. Something about the garden."

"No, I'm not psychic. It was just a lucky guess."

"You didn't feel anything in the blue room? Mollie mentioned a presence there."

"The room was cold. A tree at the window blocks the sun. I ended up sleeping in the blue room after all."

"Then why is it you've decided to write something about Arabella?" she asked bluntly.

"Proximity, I suppose. I'm a writer. I'm living at Chêne Mow. I thought it might be an interesting story. That's all."

"I'm sorry I couldn't help you, but that was all so long ago. I do have a little locket of Arabella's," she said, brightening. "My great-grandmother gave it to me. Would you like to see it?"

"I'd love to!"

"It's not the sort of thing that suits me. It's a young girl's piece. I've put it away in a desk in the study. The desk comes from Chêne Bay as well. Gordie gave it to me when he sold up the place. It's rather charming. Would you like to see it?"

"Yes, please," I said, and hopped up to follow her.

The study was a miniature of an English gentlemen's club, with oak paneling, big dark leather armchairs, and an oak desk the size of a refectory table. This was not the desk that came from Chêne Bay, however. That was a lady's desk, painted apple green, with pink flowers painted on the front. It had porcelain knobs with a brass plate behind them, matching the toilet table in the blue room at Chêne Mow. I mentioned this to Mollie.

"I noticed the toilet table was missing from Arabella's room. So that's where it's gotten to."

"Isn't it beautiful!" I exclaimed. "I want to sit down at it and write billets-doux and make romantic entries in my common book," I said, laughing at my own enthusiasm.

Emily smiled knowingly. "You sound like a Regency lady, Belle. Billets-doux and common book."

Whatever had possessed me to say that? I had never written a billet-doux in my life, and didn't have a common book.

"May I?" I asked, putting my fingers on the white knobs to pull out the drawer. I knew what it would look like inside, although I had never opened the toilet table at Chêne Mow. I could see it in my mind's eye; I could catch an echo of the woody smell. A segmented drawer, the wood a pinkish-brown color, not varnished but sanded and oiled and rubbed to a dull sheen. I was almost afraid to pull it open. I did it slowly, and found myself gazing at the drawer that had been in my head. It was an exact replica. From it came the scent of old wood. I stifled a gasp of surprise and wonder.

"The locket should be right there in that little heart-shaped box," Emily said.

I lifted the lid of a small papier-màché box painted blue, with lovebirds and hearts entwined in a flowery vine on the lid. A small golden locket on a delicate chain nestled inside. I lifted it with trembling fingers. This, too, was familiar to me at some deep, subconscious level. I knew what was in it. I eased it open with my fingernail and looked at the two locks of hair; jet black on one side, a blond curl on the other. His and hers, Arabella's. But who was he? Throckley or Vanejul?

A sudden hush invaded the room. It seemed that even breath was suspended. My heart was throbbing in my throat with excitement. My fingers closed possessively over the locket, holding on to it for dear life. I felt again that all-embracing warmth enfold me. I was afraid to open my fingers, afraid the locket would be gone. I forced myself to loosen my grip. Of course, it was still there. In a trancelike state

I fastened the trinket around my neck, lifting my hair first.

A laughing, loving voice spoke inside my head. "Damme, you'll have to do it up yourself, Belle. My fingers are too clumsy. Here, I'll hold your hair out of the way." Warm fingers brushed the nape of my neck. "There, now you have a piece of me for all eternity, or for as long as we last. You must put one of your own curls in the other side. And I shall have a piece of your mane, too, to carry next my heart."

The scissors snipped, and a blond curl fell into his waiting palm. As he wound it around his finger, a carved emerald flashed in the sunlight. At the edge of vision, I could see branches of willow drooping above a stream, like the willows at Chêne Bay. It was my phantom lover who spoke.

The next voice was an unwelcome intrusion. "The blond curl is Arabella's, according to tradition," Emily said. "I don't know who the black hair belongs to. Either Vanejul or Throckley, one assumes."

I pressed the golden charm against my flesh a moment. It fell into the hollow pocket at the base of the throat, as if it had been designed for me. Then I reluctantly unfastened the clasp and looked at it again. Emily said, and did, the most surprising thing.

"Keep it," she said. "Keep it for now. It might act as a charm to help your writing." I turned to thank her, with tears in my eyes. "It might have been made for you." She smiled a wise, arcane smile. "I thought, when I tried to put it on, that Arabella must have had a small neck, like yours."

I squeezed it tightly in my hand. "I'll take very good care of it, Emily. Thank you."

"I know you will, Belle," she said simply.

We didn't return to the morning parlor, except to pick up my purse. I left the house at once, half-afraid she would change her mind and take the locket back. I drove around the corner and parked in the dappled shade of a tree to examine my treasure. Why had Emily given it to me? Why, for that matter, did I want it so badly? It was pretty, but not outstanding. It had no diamonds, no precious stones, just the intertwined flowers engraved on the front, and the single word on the back. *Toujours.* Always.

A shudder wrenched through me. I had not turned the locket over yet. How did I know it was engraved on the back? It wasn't! It couldn't possibly be! But if it was... then time had been annihilated, and Arabella was here, confiding in me, telling me things without speaking, invading my head with her memories. Her spirit had indeed been set loose, and she had chosen me as her confidante. I was the one who was to tell her story, to free her from those nocturnal wailings in the park. I was to discover and reveal why Vanejul had killed her.

But that *toujours* was only in my mind.

I wouldn't look. I was afraid to. I felt an infinitesimal stirring of the chain in my palm. She was not going to let me act the coward. I slowly turned the heart over and read the single word, done in Gothic script. *Toujours.* That was all it said, but I knew its full meaning as well as I knew my name. It meant "we will be together always. Our love will endure forever. *Toujours.*"

The phantom voice said, "*Toujours l'amour.* How hackneyed can one get? I should be ashamed of myself. But then the truth always does sound demmed trite, don't it?" That ungrammatical "don't it?" jarred, until I remembered reading it in Byron's letters, so apparently it was a gentleman's fad of the era.

For a long time I sat in the car, trying to come to terms with the impossible thing that was happening to me. I was being lured into the beyond, to some limitless other realm never before imagined, into the enchanted boundary where sane reality blossomed into infinite eternity. The past, it seemed, was not irretrievably lost; it was poised just beyond the door of human perception, waiting, tempting, luring the unwary. But why had fate chosen me? It could hardly have chosen a less likely candidate. I was never one for taking big risks. Did I dare to venture toward this strange destiny fate had planned for me?

There was an inscrutable mystery, some unfathomable force beyond limited human comprehension at work here. Frightened as I was, I knew I could not retreat. I would continue into the unknown, with Arabella to guide me, as she had guided me to the bookstore to find Vanejul's book, and as she had guided me to Emily. With Arabella's help, I would free Arabella.

She was mine now, my responsibility, my obligation, and my opportunity. When I roused myself from the trancelike state, it was five o'clock. I must have sat there, thinking, for over an hour. I drove to the library and asked the librarian if she had any literature on Vanejul and Arabella Comstock.

She asked for references before issuing me a card. I gave Mollie and Emily, thinking they would not mind. Then she directed me to the proper department. There was no book on Arabella, but I found a large, glossy, illustrated history of the Raventhorpe family. With luck, there might be a picture of Arabella in it. As the library was closing, I had to leave without looking at the pictures.

Chapter Eight

Having accepted my fate, I felt a new calm descend upon me. I did not dash into the cottage and open the book to search for pictures of Arabella and Vanejul. I treated the book as a Christmas gift, to be savored a hundred times in imagination before opening the cover.

I made a sandwich of layers of ham shaved paper-thin, piled on crusty bread, applied a generous dollop of hot mustard. I dined on succulent green grapes from Chile, cheese from Switzerland, supped Darjeeling tea from India in my cottage in the New Forest, marveling that so many corners of the world came together in this simple cottage for this simple meal.

Only when I had removed the dishes and run water over them did I allow myself the luxury of opening the book. *The History of the Raventhorpes* was not only illustrated, it proved to be virtually a picture book, with what Sheridan describes as "a neat rivulet of text meandering through a meadow of margin."

All my characters were there: dour-faced Sir Giles Throckley with sly eyes, a prosperous belly, and a cravat up to his double chins. His son William, the man for whom Arabella had jilted Vanejul, was not my phantom lover. He was a younger, thinner, and more handsome version of Sir Giles, but with a weak chin and without the sly eyes. It was hard to credit that a sixteen-year-old lass could have fallen in love with him. But then she would have been under Sir Giles's guardianship, and he would have been at pains to put his son's interests forward.

I turned the page and gazed at Arabella. The reproduction was an oval shape, perhaps taken from one of those ivory miniatures popular in the days before the invention of the camera. It was small and the artist not a famous one, but he had caught the spirit of a gentle, pretty girl on the verge of womanhood. The blue eyes smiling at me over the centuries held a twinkle of mischief. Her full cheeks tapered to a determined little chin. Her blond hair was drawn back, with wisps of curls escaping to wanton about her cheeks. A white shawl was arranged at her shoulders. She looked about fifteen or sixteen, indicating that the likeness had been taken shortly before her death. She was not wearing the locket.

I sat a moment, communing with Arabella. Something compelled me to pick up the locket. As my fingers closed over it, I felt again that tide of sadness engulf me. Some psychics claim to read the character of the owner by holding one of the person's objects. If I had some psychic power, I wanted to use it to the full to understand Arabella. I pressed the delicate gold heart closely in my fingers and closed my eyes to concentrate.

The sadness gathered force until it sat like a rock on my chest. It slowly congealed to a burning anger, then gradually ebbed to frustration. I sat on, willing knowledge to come. The frustration increased by slow degrees to a raging fury. I could feel the mood in every atom of my being, as it swelled insensibly until I felt it consume me. *It is so unfair!* That was the message. She was with me, there in the kitchen, at the deal table, surely trying to tell me something of great moment. Then the feeling dwindled, leaving me drained.

Unable to learn more by intuition, I resorted to mere common sense. What else could she be relaying but her anger at having her life snatched away from her at such a young age? She wanted revenge on Vanejul; she wanted her life back, but that was beyond doing. All I could do was try to learn what had happened, to write it for the world to know her story, and hope that would be enough to let her troubled spirit rest.

A residue of Arabella's anger was still with me when I turned the page and saw myself gazing at my phantom lover. There he was, the handsome face, the sleek black hair, the darkly sardonic eyes, the full lips, not quite smiling. The name under it was Baron Raventhorpe, the poet Vanejul. It did not come as a surprise. An inkling of the truth had been growing inside me. Oh yes, this was the man who had had his way with a whole countryful of women. His easy charm won them without half trying, as it had no doubt won the innocent young Arabella, and he'd drowned her in the weir when she tried to escape him. This was not a face to take defeat lightly. It was accustomed to having its own way. In spite of her cruel fate, I was glad Arabella had thwarted him.

Mollie thought the ghost visiting the area was a man. If Vanejul was the force that had been called up and come to me in my dream—was it a dream?—I feared I had met more than my match. What chance had I against this demon? As I sat gazing at the book, the page showing his face flipped idly over to the next page, as pages in a tightly bound book will do. I looked at one of those meandering rivulets of print, then focused my gaze to read.

But it is all conjecture. Arabella's body was never recovered from the lake. Raventhorpe was never seen alive in England again. A local farmer reported having seen Raventhorpe argue with Arabella by the lake and throw her body into the water. The farmer was accidentally shot in the spinney by poachers the next night, shortly after giving his testimony. Some believe Raventhorpe lurked about and shot him to kill the sole witness, not knowing an affidavit had already been signed testifying to what the farmer had seen.

I turned the page back to the illustration, and sat studying the lecherous, cold-blooded murderer, wrapped up in a smiling face and disguised under a load of charm. A clever schemer who had eluded the law during his own lifetime, and historical sleuths for nearly two centuries. I felt beaten before I began. I closed the book and drew a deep sigh. I was mentally preparing an apology to Arabella when it happened.

The book flew off the table of its own volition and slammed onto the floor. There is no other way to describe it. I didn't accidentally push it. I was sitting perfectly still. There was no draft; the window was closed. No earthquake or tremor moved the floor, causing it to slide. It was hurled with a supernatural force.

I leapt up, emitting a gasp. Glancing at the window, I saw the unmistakable features of Vanejul peering in at me, and my blood turned to wax. On his face was the sardonic smile he wore in the picture. "This is all in your mind," I said out loud, trying to convince myself. Vanejul's smile stretched to a grin. He tossed his head back and laughed a soundless, mirthless laugh. Then his image faded like the Cheshire cat.

For a moment, I was incapable of movement. I stood frozen to the spot, peering from book to window, afraid that Vanejul would materialize before me and strangle me, or carry me off to the weir to join Arabella for all eternity in the cold, dark water. My heart banged against my ribs. I was afraid to stay there, and equally afraid to move. I don't know how long I would have stood there, petrified, if the door knocker had not sounded just then.

My first thought was that he was at the door seeking entrance. But Vanejul was no gentleman. He would have entered if he wished. No, he only planned to terrorize me by leering at windows, to prevent me from learning the truth. The repeated knock had an urgently human sound to it. The door opened, and before I had time to panic, Mollie's fluting voice called, "Anybody home?" Her footsteps advanced toward the kitchen. "Belle? It's me. I saw the light and thought you must be—"

Then her frizzed head appeared at the door and I ran to pitch myself into her arms. She comforted me a moment, then stood back. "Now, what is going on here?" she demanded.

"He's here! Vanejul. You did call his spirit up, Mollie, and he's come to get me. You've got to get rid of him." The words came tumbling out in a rush.

"So you've seen your first ghost," she said calmly. "Sit down and we'll have a little chat. Any chance of a cuppa?"

Eventually I settled down enough to get the tea. The cup clattered as I put it on a saucer. The tea fell uncertainly from the spout, splashing into the saucer, but I was glad to have something to do. When we were seated at the table, Mollie said, "It's nothing to be afraid of, Belle. Ghosts have no physical power. They can only get inside your head and lure you on to do things you don't want to do."

"He threw that book right off the table," I said, pointing to where it still lay on the floor.

"Then he's using a poltergeist," she said blandly. "They are a nuisance, but they're just mischief makers. What's that

75

pretty little thing?" she asked, taking up Arabella's locket.

I told her about my visit to Emily, and the trip to the library. I told her about the spirit leading me to the tobacco shop where I had found the book, and everything else that had happened to me. She listened, unfazed, totally accepting.

"He's afraid that I'm going to write Arabella's story. He wants to prevent me," I said.

She sat a moment, puzzling over this. "The world already knows, or believes, the worst of him," she pointed out.

"We don't know that. Maybe he killed other women, too. He might be a mass murderer for all we know."

"Not very likely, is it? Surely there would be a record of it if he'd killed off a whole slew of women. Perhaps he's trying to tell you something, to explain, or justify his actions. There's no real proof he killed Arabella. They dragged the lake a dozen times, but they never did find her body."

"He killed her, all right. There was a witness. Vanejul killed *him*, too, to try to prevent him from testifying."

She shook the trinket lightly in the palm of her hand. "If Vanejul is trying to accomplish something, he'll be hard to capture."

"Are you saying there's no way to get rid of him?"

"The only way is to find out what he wants, and do it."

76

I didn't smirk this time. "Then I'm leaving now. Tonight."

"Running away?" she asked, blinking her green eyes in disapproval. "Belle, I expected better of you," she chided. "This could be an unequaled chance to practice your talent."

"I'm going to phone the airport this minute," I said, and went to the phone. The phone book moved away from me as I reached for it. Mollie looked on in delight. I made another snatch, and it fell to the floor before I touched it. I picked up the receiver. It flew out of my hand.

"Vanejul wants you to stay," she said. "Don't you see what this means, Belle?"

"It means I'm getting out of here and never having anything to do with the supernatural again, ever."

Mollie picked up the telephone receiver and replaced it on the hook. Nothing tried to prevent her.

"What it could mean," she said, "is that Vanejul didn't die in Greece. He died here, at Chêne Bay. Ghosts usually return to the spot where they met their untimely end. But no, it can't be that. His fighting and dying for Greece's independence is documented. Since his mortal remains were returned to Oldstead, then that could explain his presence. He obviously has something very important to say. You can't abandon him, Belle. He deserves to have his story told, too, as well as Arabella. There must have been a reason why he killed her. You'll want to know that for your writing. The only interesting thing about her is that Vanejul loved her. Really he is the clue to her story."

The strange and incomprehensible thing is that I half wanted to stay. I was in a cold sweat at the thought of confronting Vanejul again, but I did not want to abandon Arabella. I felt that if I did, I was condemning myself to a whole future life of cowardice, to chances not dared, roads not taken.

Mollie continued her persuasions. "Come now, where is your gumption?"

"But I'm afraid!" I howled.

"Oh, pooh! Anybody would be afraid the first time. It's how you handle your fear that determines what sort of a person you are. I'll stay with you, if you like."

"Would you?"

"I'd love it. Don't be frightened. The power you possess is in all of us, but stronger in some than others. You— and I—inhabit what is called the Enchanted Boundary, that area between the visible world and the world beyond, where such wonderful things happen."

She led me to the table and filled my teacup, while talking in a calming way to soothe my fears. "I can't tell you the marvelous experiences I've had. If you leave, you'll always wonder what your life would have been if you had dared to stay. We need that touch of wonder in our lives, whether we call it religion or something else."

"I wanted to write Arabella's story," I admitted, "but how can I find out the facts at this late date?"

She studied me with a small, complacent smile. "Why don't you just write what you feel? Call it fiction. The writing will do you good, and who knows, Arabella might whisper a few truths in your ear as you write."

"You'll stay with me?"

"I have to work during the day, but it's the night's you're afraid of, isn't it? There's always something about the dark."

"Yes, so far he's only come at night."

"You'll be fine. Wear Arabella's locket. It's good to have something of hers on you, a talisman."

I put the gold chain around my neck and fastened it. I knew I was doing the right thing to stay. If any shred of common decency remained in Vanejul, he would not harm me when I was under Arabella's protection.

"If Vanejul is the ghost," I said, "then it wasn't Arabella that came at the séance, but I feel she's here, too."

Mollie looked at the necklace. "Perhaps that's what is putting you in touch with her," she said. "If both Arabella and Vanejul are around, it should be interesting."

What I was feeling was closer to terror, but from some deep well of strength within me, I summoned courage to carry on.

Chapter Nine

No visitations or nightmares disturbed my sleep in the blue room that night. In the morning, a shaft of sunlight filtered through the filigree of leaves outside my window, dappling the counterpane and walls with a mosaic of sun spots, like a Monet painting. Mollie tapped at the door and appeared with a cup of coffee in her hand.

"Mollie, you shouldn't have done that. I'm supposed to be the hostess."

"I wanted to make sure you were all right before I left, dear. I have to nip home and change. You won't be gone when I return after work, will you?"

The idea seemed absurd. I was no longer afraid, but eager to get to work. I palmed the talisman around my throat. "No, I'll be fine. I'm going to do as you suggested—just plunge in and start writing, and see what happens."

"You might be surprised," she said, setting the cup down on the table. "There's more coffee on the stove. Enjoy."

She waved and left. I plumped up the pillows and enjoyed the luxury of coffee in bed, while pondering at what point in Arabella's life I should begin her story. She would have lived a life of wealth and privilege at Chêne Bay, in that fine mansion overlooking the countryside. Her activities, however, would have been confined by the era's notions of what befitted a lady. Until they were married, young ladies were guarded like vestal virgins. That unavailability must have added to their allure. We do not value highly what we can have for the taking.

I knew from my reading of Jane Austen that the dowry was of more importance than beauty. Arabella was doubly blessed: beautiful as well as rich. Had her dowry been her main attraction for Vanejul? He would, presumably, have had wealth of his own. But then his lifestyle was no doubt extravagant. Was he a gambler, as well as a womanizer? The book had not mentioned that, but it was a common failing in those days. I had read that the Regency bucks would bet on anything, even the progress of a fly along a windowpane.

My writing wasn't to be a full biography but an account of Arabella's doings with Vanejul. I would not start at her birth, nor even at her parents' death, but at her fifteenth birthday. That was about the age at which she would have caught Vanejul's interest, and William's, and it was the part of her life that interested me—especially her murder by Vanejul.

I finished the coffee, washed up, and slid into jeans and a clean shirt. It was a white shirt of my dad's that was too small for him and really too large for me, but it was my security blanket. I always felt he was looking out for me when I wore it. An odd fancy, that. Had I always had an intimation of some invisible power lurking at the periphery of normal life? I made the bed and ran down to the kitchen. Breakfast was the rest of the grapes, a bun, and another cup of coffee.

When I went to the typewriter, it seemed wrong. The banging of the keys against the platen disturbed me, although it hadn't before. My fingers kept striking the wrong keys. A pen seemed the proper writing tool. I got out a fresh sheet of typewriter paper, unfortunately not lined, and began to write. I would begin on Arabella's fifteenth birthday, June 9, 1800, according to the book. And I would put her at the only spot at Chêne Bay I knew well, the weir. When I closed my eyes, I could almost see her there, an innocent young girl-woman, warm and happy in the sunlight of her youth. I wrote:

The fruit trees were in bloom at Chêne Bay on that lovely day in June. They looked like giant balls of cotton wool against the azure sky. Arabella felt grown-up in her pink sprigged muslin gown. Her new kid slippers had a small heel, and a silver buckle that winked in the sunlight as her feet flew over the park, down to the stream.

Her hired companion, Mrs. Meyers, had given her a new netting box for her birthday, despite repeated hints for a pair of blue silk stockings seen in Allyson's Drapery Shop. Mrs. Meyers was a good woman, but sadly lacking in romance. She would not have let herself fall into flesh at forty years, and she would not have worn those horrid old gray gowns, if she had any notion of romance. In her hand Arabella carried the present Cousin William had given her, a copy of Mr. Wordsworth's poems. But Uncle Throckley had given the best present of all. He was having a rout party that evening, with all the young ladies and gentlemen of the neighborhood coming to honor her birthday.

"Now that you are all grown-up, it is time to introduce you to the young gentlemen. Mind you don't let any of them steal your heart away," Uncle Throckley added waggishly. "We don't want to lose you yet, do we, William?" He leveled a commanding eye at his chinless son.

"No indeed, Papa," William replied dutifully.

The whole household was in on the secret of the party; for days the servants had been preparing raised pies and hams and macaroons. They had turned out the whole downstairs of Chêne Bay. The carpets were lifted and hung over the clothesline and beaten; beeswax and turpentine were applied to the furnishings, and even the windows were cleaned with vinegar and water.

"Spring cleaning, missy," Mrs. Meyers had said in her stern way when Arabella inquired why these unusual exertions were going forth. But it had all been for her party. The world seemed a delicious place to Arabella that morning.

I wrote like a demon for two hours, filling page after page, while the coffee grew cold in my cup. The pictures were all there in my head, of Arabella's excited little face, and the sprigged muslin gown with the high waist. I could feel her excitement pulsing through my veins as the words came pouring out. William Throckley joined her in the park, and tried to steal a kiss behind the cherry tree. I felt her fearful excitement, and knew it was her first kiss. I knew, too, that while she was disappointed at the lack of fervor, she was not repelled by the experience. She liked William then. And she was a passionate creature.

I followed her through her day. She received three letters wishing her a happy birthday, and read them at her desk, the little apple green desk now in Emily's study. In the afternoon, Arabella and Mrs. Meyers, that stout, unimaginative lady with a heart of marshmallow, drove into Lyndhurst and had an ice, then examined the wares in Allyson's Drapery Shop. In vain the eager owner had brought down the ells of muslin and contraband silk to tempt the heiress. Arabella bought only new blue ribbons for her hair. The villagers bowed and smiled at the young heiress. Her gentleness had won her a place in their hearts.

At eleven I stopped only long enough to stretch my cramped limbs and have a glass of juice, then I returned to my writing. I felt Arabella was with me. Quaint words whose meaning I scarcely knew were appearing on those pages. Words like *reticule* and *pelisse*, meaning purse and cloak. The writing had put me in touch with that deep well of memory amassed over years of reading. This had been a wonderful idea of Mollie's.

She was right to urge me to stay and develop my talent, for I felt, deep inside, that what I was writing was not just imagination. It was what had happened on that June day nearly two hundred years ago. I felt fifteen years old, with all the trembling wonder of a child becoming a woman. I did not feel shackled by the constraints placed on Arabella as I would if I were required to have a companion for a run into the village. It seemed natural and right.

The boundaries of time were blurred, allowing me to sense past happenings as if they had been recorded in some magical element into which I had access. I was a part of the past, while still living in the twentieth century. I was a part of the universal wisdom of the ages. I even had a glimmering of why Fate, or Arabella, had chosen me as her intermediary, despite my timidity of the unknown. Why was I timid, unless I was afraid of it? And if I was afraid, then I believed. That, I felt, was the sine qua non of being chosen. One had to believe or be capable of belief in unseen forces.

Two days ago I would have called myself a nonbeliever, but after recent occurrences, I was open to doubts. The writing continued at a feverish pace.

The hour of the rout party drew near. Arabella donned a white deb's gown, trimmed around the ruched skirt with small silken rosebuds. At her ears she wore pearl teardrop pendants. She went, proudly but shyly, down the gracefully curving staircase of Chêne Bay to take her place at the door of the ballroom with her uncle Throckley and William, to be presented to society as a new belle. A pressure was building in her as the guests began to come forward to be greeted. Her eyes flickered down the waiting line, assessing the ladies' toilettes and the gentlemen's faces, until she met the sardonic gaze of Lord Raventhorpe. Then her heart began to flutter out of control.

His jet black head towered proudly six inches above the country squires and their wives. At this throat he wore an immaculate cravat, arranged in intricate folds. The jacket on his shoulders fit as smoothly as the skin on a peach. While he waited, inching forward in the line, his sloeberry eyes never left Arabella's face. They gazed on her unblinkingly, until she blushed in annoyed pleasure. She thought him bold— but so handsome! She must not encourage him. Miss Meyers said he was fast. She said Uncle Throckley ought not to have invited him, but then he was visiting the Percivals, and one could hardly not invite such old friends as the Percivals.

After five minutes that seemed a decade, he was bowing with easy grace over Arabella's fingers. He lifted her hand to his lips, stopping the ritual inch away from them. At the touch of his warm fingers, the fluttering in her breast increased to a pounding so loud, she feared he could hear it. No one else had done that! No one else gazed at her with such blatant admiration. When he spoke, his dark eyes scrutinized her face, darting from hair to eyes to lips. His accent was the honeyed silk of the gazetted flirt.

"Why have I not seen you before, Miss Comstock?" he asked. His intimate smile made it the grandest compliment she had ever received.

With the safety of her uncle by her side, she replied, "You have seen me often, sir. In fact, your curricle splashed mud on my skirt not a month ago, in Lyndhurst. You were driving much too quickly!" she chided.

"It is my way to proceed a little more quickly than society likes," he said. His smile gave the words a world of meaning. "If you will give me the opportunity, I shall apologize, and even buy you a new..." He gave a diffident little laugh. "But that would be farouche. Shall I be farouche? No," he said, glancing unconcernedly at Sir Giles, "I think not. You will save me a set of waltzes, Miss Comstock?"

"I don't waltz, sir."

"Ah! Then at least I shall not suffer the agony of seeing you in some other man's arms."

"You *are* fast, Lord Raventhorpe," Arabella said, trying to maintain her dignity, but an encouraging smile peeped out.

"We have already discussed that, ma'am. Let us not reheat old news. We can—and shall—find more interesting things to talk about—like your sweet self." He bowed and moved on to shake William's hand, while Arabella stood, feeling as if she had grown up from a girl to a lady in those two minutes.

Uncle Throckley whispered in her ear, "You don't want to have much to do with young Raventhorpe. He's a bad 'un."

It was already too late. The arrow had hit its mark. The rout party proceeded apace, but while Arabella performed the stately minuet with William, her mind and her heart were with Raventhorpe. It stung like a nettle to see him flirting his head off with Miss Summers. He ignored Arabella for three quarters of the evening. He had the cotillion with Amy Peters, the romping country dance with Mary Holmes, and by suppertime, Arabella was so angry, she planned to refuse when—if—he asked her to dance.

He took Mary Holmes in to supper, but positioned himself in such a manner that he could, and did, observe Arabella throughout. She would look up from her lobster patties to see his dark eyes studying her. On his face was a small, patient smile, which told her he was biding his time.

When he came directly to her after supper, her anger had transmuted to a wild excitement. "You're angry with me" were his first words. "I am so glad. That means you care, a little."

"I don't care a brass farthing," she retorted.

"Yes, you do. You should have feigned indifference if you wanted me to think otherwise. And I care that you care. I could not make it obvious that I am enchanted with you, or Sir Giles would lock you in your room. That would not stop me from seeing you, but it would be deuced awkward. I'd rather meet you in a less mischievous place than your boudoir. Shall we say, by the weir?"

She listened, with her heart pitter-pattering excitedly. "When did you have in mind? Not that I'll be there."

"After sunset would be best."

"A dark night for dark deeds, sir?" she asked, with a flirtatious glance.

He smiled lazily. "Preferably a moonlit night. I want to be able to see you. You are something quite out of the ordinary, you know. Did anyone ever tell you, you have eyes like sapphires?"

"Several times."

"I thought as much, which is why I shan't bore you with a repetition. Your eyes are nothing like sapphires. Nor is your skin like marble or satin or a peach, nor your hair like gold silk. These vegetables and mineral comparisons are poor stuff when you come down to it."

"Could you do better?"

"I could, but it takes a moonlit night to inspire me. Will you come to the weir after the party?"

"Certainly not."

"Very well, but I shall be there, filling the lake with my tears. When Chêne Bay is ten feet underwater and the whole land flooded, then you'll regret your cruelty, madam."

She laughed in spite of herself. "You are too ridiculous, milord."

"Beautiful ladies make fools of us all. I do believe it is why God invented you, to provide Himself a chuckle at man's absurdity from time to time." He spoke facetiously, but his eyes were anxious when he said, "Do come. You know perfectly well Sir Giles won't welcome me at the house. He has been looking daggers at me all evening."

"If your reputation is so black as that, I don't think I ought to see you again," she said, but she said it with an encouraging smile.

"It is not my reputation, but his son's lack of address, that frightens him. If he ever let a real man next or nigh you, William would have no chance of attaching you."

"William happens to be a very good friend of mine."

"That alone condemns him to ineligibility. A friend indeed! When did a young miss ever have the sense to marry a friend? When did a gentleman either, for that matter? I am not just denigrating your sex, Miss Comstock. No, what the ladies want is a corsair."

"And what do the gentlemen want?"

"Oh, we are not fussy. We demand only beauty, breeding, a fortune—and enough reluctance on the lady's part to let us fondly imagine we have won her over all odds, after she has landed us."

"I shouldn't think the reluctance would be hard to come by, if this is the way you carry on."

Their conversation was frequently interrupted by the steps of the dance. It lent a certain piquancy to the conversation, having to wait for an answer. Arabella had time to wonder what Raventhorpe meant by intimating Sir Giles wished her to marry William. Sir Giles had never suggested a match between them. When she was swung back into Raventhorpe's arms, he said, "Don't leave me on the rack, you cruel woman. What is it to be? Will you meet me by the weir?"

"Not tonight," she said.

"I plan to leave tomorrow."

91

She gave a pouting shrug. "Then you are obviously not serious. Why should I risk my reputation for a man who is literally here tonight, gone tomorrow?"

"I shall return, Arabella. I will always return. I have been suborned into accompanying Mrs. Percival to Oldstead Abbey tomorrow, but it is only ten miles away. I would crawl on my knees, if necessary. I was quite serious about men's absurdity, you see."

That night Arabella slipped out of the house after the household was asleep and met Raventhorpe by the weir. It was the first of many trysts.

As I finished a page, I flicked it aside and drew forward a blank sheet. Glancing up, I was astonished to see the welter of pages littering the table. Had I really written all that? It was my writing, but in my haste I had scrawled so badly, it was hard to read. I, who usually brooded over every sentence, had filled two dozen sheets. What time was it? I looked at my watch, and could hardly believe it was six-thirty.

Mollie would be returning soon, and I had not made a single plan for dinner. I'd have to serve eggs, which didn't seem much reward for her help. The whole idea of Mollie coming seemed an intrusion. I would have to waste the evening entertaining her, when I wanted to continue with Arabella's story. I was on thorns to see what I would write.

The phone jangled. When I picked up the receiver, Mollie said, "Hi, Belle. It's me. How are things going?"

"Fine. Very well."

"Good. What do you say you drive into Lyndhurst and meet me for a bite in town? I have to show a customer a house at eight o'clock. We could go to the cinema after, or have a couple of ales at the pub."

"I'm busy, Mollie. I'd rather not tonight. You go ahead."

"Will you be all right there alone after dark?" she asked.

"Yes, I'm fine. I don't mind at all. It's all right now."

"No—ahem—visitors?" she asked archly.

"No visitors."

"If you're sure, I'll show Duggan the house and be there around nine-thirty. I'll stop by my place and pack a bag."

I'd be written out by nine, and would be glad to have Mollie here overnight. It was selfish, but Arabella had become so important to me that I was willing to be selfish on her behalf. "That'll be fine, Mollie. Thanks a lot."

"Ta ta for now, then."

"'Bye." I hung up and went back to the table. In my wild burst of scribbling, I hadn't kept the pages in any sort of order, but the most recently written ones should have been on top. What sat on top was the first page. I stared in disbelief. The page was vibrating slightly, as if a breeze were disturbing it, but there was no breeze. I felt a warmth at my back. Without turning, I knew he was there, in the room with me. I waited for fear to seize me, but felt only a rising excitement untouched by dread or fear.

Chapter Ten

Raventhorpe—Vanejul—my phantom lover—leaned over the scattered sheets of manuscript, and I trembled with joy. At first the vision was insubstantial, no more than the shimmering uncertainty of one's own reflection seen in the window of a lighted room at night. As I stared, the apparition became more solid, until at last he looked completely normal, as if made of flesh and blood. His presence hardly seemed odd, after having spent the whole day with him in imaginings more vivid than any reality I had ever known.

The well-remembered sloeberry eyes, black and luminous, looked up from the page, smiling in pleasure at what I had written. "You are a little confused," he said, "but then it was a long time ago. Sir Giles had the coming-out party in May, before her birthday. The trees had lost their blossoms by June."

I had some idea how a naive, fifteen-year-old Belle had felt when she was first confronted with this overpowering presence. How excited she must have been by his handsome masculinity, how intimidated by his title and arrogance, and how flattered, withal, that he honored her with his attentions. I shared every atom of her excitement, and had to brace myself to meet him on an equal footing. I was no naive teenager raised in the nineteenth century. I didn't need Vanejul. If what Mollie had said was true, he needed me, yet I felt an instinctive feminine urge to please him. This would not do!

"Then Arabella was only fourteen. Practically a child," I said accusingly. It seemed ludicrous that this man should have been interested in a teenager. He looked to be in his early thirties—a man capable of dealing with Cleopatra, or the Queen of Sheba. Of course, he had been younger when he met Arabella. This must be the body he had when he died in Greece. The age looked right, and Greece's climate could account for the swarthiness of his complexion.

"She was at the tag end of her fifteenth year. Older than Juliet," he pointed out, not apologetically, but with an air of incipient annoyance. "Many young ladies married at fifteen or sixteen. This modern notion of delaying marriage a decade is unhealthy. Nature knows what she is about. To pitch two unchaperoned youngsters together, chock-full of raging hormones, and then express outrage when they do what comes naturally—it is blatant hypocrisy."

95

I agreed, but did not say so. "The world has changed from your day, Vanejul."

"Customs have changed, but not human nature. In any case, you traduce me to imply I was preying on a child. Arabella knew what she was about."

"I didn't mean to imply that. Anyway, it's only a story."

"If you're going to tell our story, get it right," he said boldly. "You'll look nohow if you don't even know when the trees blossom."

"At home, they blossom in late May. They could still be in bloom in early June."

"The tragedy didn't happen in America," he pointed out. "It happened here. Do more than just think how it might have been, Belle. You are a young woman. Put yourself in her head, feel what she felt," he said persuasively.

His charm was working its spell. I must be careful with this man. "I am," I replied. "I know exactly how she felt."

"Really?" He gave a curious, disillusioned look. "And did she truly love me—ever?" He waited, gazing deeply into my eyes, with a hungry look about him.

"She was fascinated."

His elegant hands moved in dissatisfaction. The carved emerald flashed. "Fascination is a fleeting sort of emotion, based on appearance, or inexperience, or a childish misconception that someone can fill a romantic need. One grows out of a mere fascination. I know she was fascinated. I asked you if she loved me," he said brusquely.

"I don't know her well enough yet. I have just begun the story."

"I half dread to know the truth."

He looked again at my manuscript. "This bit about my splashing her in my curricle. I wasn't even driving the demmed thing. My tiger was. I told her that. You make me sound overbearing."

A smile twitched at my lips. "Fancy that! I imagined a flaw in you, and here you thought you were perfect."

He cocked his head to one side. I watched as a devastating smile stretched across his lips and lit his eyes. "Modesty never was my long suit. But then I hadn't much to be modest about. Put that in your book, if you dare. Draw me warts and all—and Belle, too. Let posterity decide which of us is the villain of the piece."

I should have despised that remark, but there is some charm in self-love, when it is lightened with humor. "I shall do my best. Any other complaints?"

He lifted his shapely hand, palms up, in a gesture of apology. "Forgive me. I am a savage, chiding you when you are kind enough to do this for me. I do appreciate it. I've waited so long..." He emitted a weary little sigh.

"I'm doing it for Arabella."

"For both of us." He nodded, satisfied to share the story with her.

It began to seem like any visit with a particularly exciting friend. I felt he was my friend, despite my knowledge of his history. He had that way with women. I drew my chair to sit down but hesitated a moment. I nearly offered him a cup of tea, till I remembered in time that he had no physical powers. Oh, but his emotional force was formidable. I must heed Mollie's warning about letting him inside my head, to make me do things I should not. Already I was mentally scanning what I had written, to see if I had been unconsciously whitewashing Arabella, or maligning Vanejul.

His eyes toured my body from head to toes in that age-old way of a man sizing up a woman. Then a frown puckered his brow. "Why the devil do you wear trousers?" he asked.

"All the women wear them nowadays. They're comfortable. Don't you like them?"

"They're ugly," he said bluntly. "If God had wanted women to wear trousers—"

"He would have given us two legs?"

A reckless grin flashed out. "Touché. What I meant, but was a little shy to say, is that He would not have given you such prominent... er, that is to say." I felt myself blush as he examined my prominent posterior. Despite the objection, his interest did not seem unduly critical. Rather otherwise. "And the shirt, too. You look quite the little guy," he said, and put his hands on my chair, but of course, he couldn't draw it for me.

"I'm working on the prominent thing," I murmured, seating myself. Raventhorpe remained standing.

"Don't." It was less than a command, more than a request. "Just wear a dress next time. It is more feminine and alluring. I don't understand the contemporary she. You starve and batter your poor bodies to skin and bones, then drape them in monstrous shirts that hide it all. Can you explain this mystery to me?"

"We call it being in shape. It's good for you."

"It is no favor to men, to burden our imaginations with inventing a body for you."

"Fashions change. The contemporary male prefers slender women."

"At least that has not changed. I am heartened to hear all your self-inflicted punishment is to please us. I venture to say you misunderstand the male mind. Men have never objected to feminine women. Between losing your figures and your skirts, you put the onus of sexual attraction on the men. But then it is so in nature, *vide* the peacock and the lion."

"Was Arabella plump?" I asked, to direct his attention away from the body and clothes that did not please him.

"She was—perfect. Or so I thought, but then I never saw a flaw when I was in love."

"You did truly love her then, at the beginning?"

He looked confused and hurt that I

should ask. "At the beginning? Longer than that, Belle. Until she would not let me love her."

"Until she fell in love with William, you mean?"

"William was not the cause of her change, but one of the effects." He shook his head, as though to dispel a bitter memory. When he spoke again, it was of other things. He glanced at the typewriter. "That's an infernal machine. I am glad I could convince you to ignore it. Nothing mechanical should come between the artist and her thoughts."

He had convinced me? The man's conceit was incredible. "How did you write? Cut the end of your finger and write in blood? A pencil's mechanical."

"You take me too literally, my pet. I meant you should stick to the minimum of interference. The clatter of that contraption would deafen an auctioneer. I, if you are really interested and not just being satirical, used a quill first, then a patent pen. You're very prolific, Belle," he continued, gesturing to the written pages. "I was told by my publisher, that's John Murray, that I wrote too much. I never could bother to recobble my outpourings, pasting on a simile here and a quotation there. I daresay I was overly prolific, though my readers managed to keep up with me."

I felt a thrill at that casual "my pet," and

braced myself against him. "I don't much care for your Grecian and Italian poetry," I said sternly.

His brows lowered and his lips thinned. "That wasn't poetry. It was literary bile. I am surprised you choose to dredge up that particular subject."

"It compromises three quarters of your output."

"Whose fault is that?" he asked roughly.

"Yours. If you'd spent less time whoring and more time with your patent pen—"

He flung an angry arm into the air. "By God, if this don't beat all! I thought you were my friend, my redeemer. If you only mean to hack and hammer at what remains of my poor reputation, go back where you came from—or you will be very sorry, madam," he said, finishing on a tone of silken menace that sent a shiver up my spine.

This was the first I had seen of the infamous Raventhorpe temper. It was a little frightening, and after all, I had only said the truth. "It's only a story," I repeated.

"Yes, a story about a lady called Arabella Comstock, of Chêne Bay, and a gent called Raventhorpe. It stretches the long arm of coincidence to suggest it is all make-believe."

"I shall probably change the names before I send it to a publisher."

"In other words, you've no imagination. You've come here to plunder my story, and Arabella's, and palm it off as your own idea. Why, I shouldn't be surprised to see you hammer on a happy ending. By God, that would be the ultimate irony." His arms flayed the air angrily. "If that's all you're good for, I shan't help you anymore."

"Arabella is helping me," I said airily. My fingers went to the locket, fingering it as a talisman.

As his dark eyes followed the movement of my fingers, his little burst of anger faded. I sensed that he was the volatile sort who flared up like a fire rocket and soon settled back down. For a fleeting moment, a small, vulnerable boy peered out from his eyes. "I see you got hold of the locket. Are our locks of hair still in it?"

So the hair was his! "Yes."

"I'd like to see them."

I removed it and held it out. He reached, as if he would like to hold it, then glanced unhappily at his hands. I held it out to him. "It's your hair, then? I thought it might be William's, but his hair looked lighter in the picture."

"William's! Why would she keep that mawworm's hair in the locket I gave her?" His voice was rough with anger, or perhaps with regret. It was hard to say. "Light and dark—we used to joke it was a symbol of our natures." It was regret, and infinite longing. His sad eyes would draw pity from a rock. "I, it hardly needs saying, was the dark one, Arabella the light. Vain creature."

"Tell me about her death," I said. The words came unbidden. I hadn't meant to ask him, not while he was in such an uncertain mood at least.

His regret hardened to a sneer. "You ask all the wrong questions, ma'am. Ask, rather, what she did with her life. What other hearts did she break, besides mine? Look in your own heart, if you have one, and see who was truly wronged in this piece of 'fiction' you are plagiarizing from my life."

"Tell me," I repeated, untouched by his anger.

"Who cares how she died? We all must die. How we live is the important matter, and she lived badly. I'll tell you this, there never would have been a Vanejul if Arabella had not—" He stopped in frustration. "No, I shan't say it. I shan't accuse her of such a wicked piece of perfidy until I know for sure what happened."

"You mean you don't know! But you are the one who—" I stopped short of accusing him of murder, because I was afraid. "No one can harm you now. It's all done and over with. You must tell me." My voice was brusque with eagerness.

"You think I hastened her demise?" Again he cocked his head to one side in a playful manner. "Doesn't everyone kill the thing he loves, one way or another? If not an actual physical death, then spiritually. I know she stopped loving me," he said, in a voice schooled to indifference, but his pain showed through the mask, like old paint on a cracked painting, with a darker picture behind it. "That was the beginning of Vanejul. But for that, I might have been a real poet. I only wrote that claptrap to punish her, to show her how little I cared. I frittered away whatever talent I had on those puerile pieces."

"They're not that bad," I said softly, to ease his pain.

"I am ashamed to admit authorship of them. I chose her name for those angry works, so that she alone would know the author. I could not like to sully my family name with such literary sludge. 'Vain jewel' was a pet name I used to call her. Hazlitt, that louse on the locks of literature—I am indebted to Lord Tennyson for the delightful phrase—invented the notion that I was rearranging the spelling of Juvenal, perhaps because he, too, was a satirist and a poet."

"And a woman-hater."

He looked astonished. "I never was that! *Au contraire*. I enjoyed women only too well."

"A telling phrase. I expect you enjoy beefsteak, too, and horses and—"

"Point made." He executed an exquisite little bow. "I should have said I appreciate women."

"Only too well!"

He colored slightly, and immediately changed the subject. "With regard to Juvenal, there was the exile, too, and the military career. A few points in common.

At least I concur with his reason for writing satire. When asked, he replied, 'How could I help it?' I doubt he had as much reason as I."

"Was she in love with William? Was that what happened?"

After a frowning pause, he said, "She liked him at first. I thought, toward the end, she loathed him quite as thoroughly as I did. But there were twists in the girl I never began to understand. As I said, William was only a pawn in the game. She used him to punish me."

"For what?"

"For loving her. That was my sin."

"That doesn't make sense."

"No, it doesn't, does it? I have been brooding over that enigma for centuries." He looked at his hands, and frowned. "Damme, I'm fading."

I was thoroughly shocked to see that it was the case. He was disappearing before my very eyes. I had forgotten that he was not actually flesh and blood.

"Don't go! I want to ask you a hundred things."

I leapt up from the table and tried to hold on to him. It was like trying to hold smoke. He was gone. The spot where he had been was cold. I thought, or imagined, a sigh of regret as he departed.

A feeling of utter fatigue came over me as an aftermath of my busy day and the meeting with Raventhorpe. I regretted that I had not put the meeting to better use.

I hadn't discovered the answers I needed for my book. I had been too fascinated by the man. The trees blossoming out of season was a mere detail. But as I reviewed our meeting, I realized that he seemed to take my story for an actual account of his relationship with Arabella. Had the rout party really occurred, if not then, at an earlier date?

Was Arabella the true author of this book? A nice moral question, as I planned to put my name on it. I made a pot of tea and a cheese sandwich and read over the hastily scrawled pages. It was as though I were reading them for the first time. Really they didn't sound like my writing at all. What was a rout party, for heaven's sake? And a curricle? He spoke as if he had truly splashed Arabella with his curricle.

When I returned the locket to my neck, I felt just a slight intimation of warm fingers assisting me. Was it Arabella, or was he still here, in some invisible form? How interesting if I could get them both to come at the same time, and hear why she had jilted him. After having met him, that was the greatest mystery of all.

Would he ever come back? When I realized how very much I wanted him to return, I drew myself up short. This man had murdered Arabella. He tried to weasel out of answering me, but the facts spoke for themselves. After having met him, I understood how she had fallen so quickly and easily under his spell. What I could not fathom was how she could ever have jilted him. There must have been an over-powering reason. Infidelity? That would have enraged her, but I felt he could charm even that transgression away. The man was an enchanter. Had he seduced her? But that would more or less force her to marry him, in those days. Perhaps his violent temper had been his undoing. Had he struck her, or made threats? He had threatened me. *You will be very sorry, madam.*

I was happy Mollie was coming to spend the night with me, but I decided against sharing this latest adventure with her. I wanted to hug the secret to myself a lit-tle longer. When she returned, I told her I was writing Arabella's story, but said not a word about Vanejul. Vain jewel. He found Arabella vain, then, as well as a precious jewel. That would not bother him; he was no stranger to vanity himself.

"I sold Duggan the house!" Mollie smiled. "Lovely commish for me! And how was your day, dear?"

"The story went well."

"No ghosties came to visit?" she asked playfully.

"I felt Arabella was guiding my hand," I prevaricated, "but she didn't make an appearance."

"Shall we turn on the telly? I heard Raventhorpe's taken a turn for the worse. He might be dead by now. Not that it'll make any difference to our ghost, but it makes the case interesting somehow. The past and the present all mixed up."

We watched the news. Raventhorpe was not dead, but had recovered somewhat. It showed a tape of him at Ascott a few years before, but the picture was not clear. I could see he was tall and well enough built, with some trace of his ancestor's charm in his smile.

"Since Vanejul had no son and heir, who inherited the title?" I asked Mollie.

"It was a cousin. A forgettable man. None of the rest of the family are poets. A pity Vanejul hadn't had a son."

"I imagine Italy and Greece were littered with by-blows. Little Fitz-Vanejuls, if he acknowledged them at all."

"I don't suppose he did, though. Shall we have a cuppa before bed?"

We had tea and toast, and went to bed early. Exhausted, I sank into a deep sleep. After thinking of Vanejul and Arabella all day, it was natural that I should dream of them. But was it normal that the book should continue writing itself while I slept? This robbed me of any control, and frightened me when I awoke in the morning with the memory of my night's doings. But then what could be considered normal in the whole affair? I had passed far beyond normalcy, into another realm. I had allowed myself to take the great leap into the unknown, and now I must ride the whirlwind.

Chapter Eleven

Mollie continued on with me for a few days. I have some vague memory of her comings and goings, but very little recall of her actually being in the house. I remember her worried eyes peering out from that halo of Titian frizz, asking me if I was all right when she returned from work. When I assured her I was, she must have gone out again, since I wrote in the evenings, too, and I would not have done so if Mollie had been there. Most of my waking hours were spent in a frenzied storm of writing, writing, writing. It seemed of the greatest urgency that I write the tale Arabella revealed to me as I sat at the deal table, mindless of the spring sunshine at the window, of the sink filling with dishes, of the world beyond the cottage.

Sappho stopped in the second afternoon about three and invited me into town with her. She looked stunning in a simple black dress, very tight to show off her well-toned body, and short to reveal her shapely legs. She was wearing red sandals. A black kerchief with white polka dots the size of half dollars hid her hair, but revealed enormous gypsy earrings.

"I'll show you the best places to shop," she said. "You want to avoid the tourist traps on the main street. Their prices are exorbitant in the summer."

"It sounds tempting, but I'm pretty busy at the moment, Sappho. Thanks anyway for the offer." I could hardly take my eyes from my work, even to thank her.

Undismayed and uninvited, she sat down at the table, picked up a sheet, and began glancing at what I had written. "Emily mentioned you're doing an article on Vanejul and Arabella," she said. "Must be a long article."

"It seems to be turning into a novel. It's just loosely based on the story, since I couldn't find out much about her."

She lifted her witch black eyes from the page and smiled coolly. "So I see. I suggest you not use the names Vanejul and Arabella at all. You're quite off the track, to judge by this bit." She tossed the page aside.

"What do you mean?"

"You haven't given this much thought, Belle. This tragedy occurred in the early eighteen hundreds, when girls were reared like nuns. They weren't allowed out unchaperoned. You know what Vanejul was like." Her eyes slid to the paperback I'd bought in Lyndhurst. "You've read his poetry. He despised women. In every poem the woman jilts him, and he takes revenge. He was a rake."

"That's not how it was!" I said angrily.

"That's obviously not how you think it was. A biographer shouldn't fall in love with her subject. It distorts her objectivity. Arabella's guardian wouldn't have let a man like Vanejul within a country mile of her."

"Are you saying they never met?"

"No, they lived near each other. I think Vanejul was probably chasing after her. When she paid no attention to him, he arranged one of his little tricks, the sort of thing he did so well in Italy. He lured her to a quiet spot and had his way with her. He always took what he wanted. After he'd raped her, he could hardly set her free. That's why he drowned her and fled to Greece."

"Don't be ridiculous!" I scoffed, but she had cast a shadow on my hero.

His later poems did reveal a deep-seated dislike of women. His conversation had reinforced it. When I asked him if he loved Arabella, he had said something about "until she would not let me love her." What did that mean? And when he opened the locket he said, "Light and dark... a symbol of our natures. I, it hardly needs saying, was the dark one." Other fragments of our conversation echoed inside my head. "Who cares how she died? We all must die." Surely that was not the voice of love speaking. If he had killed her as Sappho said, naturally he would not want me to harp on it.

When I tuned back in to the present, Sappho was gazing at the locket. "Did Emily give you that?" she asked sharply.

Since she had recognized it, I had to admit how I had come by it. "She lent it to me."

"And filled your head with her notions of clairvoyance. There's a difference between clairvoyance and imagining. Poor Emily. She's really past it. Well, if you don't want to go shopping, I'll be off. Think about what I told you, Belle," she said, with a pat on my shoulder. Then she picked up her big black patent purse and went out, leaving her poison behind her.

I couldn't help thinking about it. What she had suggested was not implausible by any means. She had tarnished Vanejul's luster for me. I began examining his writings with a more critical eye, wondering.... Then I examined my own story. Had I been whitewashing Vanejul's behavior? Perhaps what troubled me most of all was Sappho's charge that I was falling in love with my subject. The visit put me off my stride. Before I returned to work, the phone rang. It was Emily.

"How are you coming along with your story, Belle?" she asked.

I told her about Sappho's visit, and its effect on my writing.

"Pay her no heed. Just wear the locket and listen to your heart. I suppose Sappho saw the locket?"

"Yes."

"She must wonder why I gave you such a valuable thing. She knows, of course, that I'm psychic. I had my reasons," she said

112

mysteriously. "I only hope I did the right thing."

We talked a little longer. Mollie had told her she was staying with me. "If you're frightened there at night, I'll send my dog over to guard you."

I pictured a Doberman pinscher, and felt I'd rather take my chances with a burglar. "What kind of dog is it?"

"Beezle's a poodle. He wouldn't hurt a flea, but he has a good loud bark. He'd alert you if you had a prowler. I'll ask Henry to delivery him. He's bringing me some vegetables from his farm this afternoon."

I knew I couldn't impose on Mollie all summer, and thanked Emily for the loan of Beezle. A small dog would be company.

Henry Thorndyke delivered the poodle later that afternoon in a truck that looked about fifty years old. Emily had sent some cans of dog food, a feeding schedule, and a basket for Beezle to sleep in. Beezle wasn't clipped into strange puffs and balls, but wore a full, curly coat of hair. He seemed to be friendly. I played with him for a while, to become acquainted.

I tried to write, but no inspiration came. Sappho had done her job too well. I spent an hour cleaning the house, washing dishes, dusting, trying to exorcize the demons in my mind. When I could find no more dust or dirty dishes, I decided to take Beezle out for a walk.

When Mollie returned around six, we had

dinner together, and caught up on the day's doings.

"Sappho dropped in. Oh, and Emily called." I told her about the trouble I was having with my writing after Sappho's visit.

"You look peaky, dear. Why don't you go upstairs and have a lie-down. I'll clean up after dinner."

I didn't come back downstairs that night. At about ten, Mollie came up to see if I was all right. She insisted on heating a can of soup for me. I ate half of it, then felt so tired, I just turned out the light and went back to sleep. I had a horrible night of tossing and turning and dreaming. In my dream, I was looking for Vanejul.

I was in a dark labyrinth, a sort of maze of passageways and blind alleys, made of soaring, funereal yews. Sharp branches clutched at my gown and pricked my bare arms as I scurried along the endless corridors, looking for Vanejul. I wore a long, white gown, and as if in two places, I could look down from above and see myself, hurrying like a mouse through the maze. Yet my view from above was no help in negotiating the twists and turns of the passage.

At times I caught a glimpse of Vanejul, who would look over his shoulder, to see I was following. I could not tell whether he was luring me on or trying to escape me. He would seem to hesitate at corners, as if to wait for me, but when I hurried forward, he was gone. Once I thought I had him. He turned another corner, and when I reached it, I saw it was one of the blind alleys. But when I looked all around, he was nowhere to be seen. He had magically evaporated into thin air.

The yews grew densely together, right to the ground. He could not have crawled through the hedge to another corridor. I stopped in frightened confusion. My heart, or my conscience, said in an imperious voice, *This is what comes of chasing after phantoms.* It was not so much a warning as an indictment. I had broken some divine law, and was condemned to spend eternity in this dark maze.

Then the voice faded, and from the other side of the yew hedge, I heard Vanejul's low chuckle. He was not laughing at me. The teasing quality of his laughter suggested he was with a woman, and I was consumed with a burning rage. Then another voice spoke, a soft voice, in that same teasing way. The rage withered to frustration, to despair. He was with Sappho!

"Raventhorpe!" I called through the hedge. "Come and save me. I'm lost. It's Arabella. Come. Come away. Raventhorpe. Raventhorpe." My wails diminished to a whine.

I felt a light jostling on my arm, and when I opened my eyes, Mollie's worried face was gazing down at me.

"Wake up, Belle. You're having a bad dream," she said. "I've brought you some breakfast. Just toast and an egg. Are you all right?"

She had raised the blinds, or I had forgotten to close them. Daylight flooded the blue room. It danced on the counterpane and made my head ache.

"I'm all right. Thanks, Mollie."

She felt my forehead and shook her head. "I don't like to leave you."

"Don't be silly. You have to go to work. I'll be fine."

She left, and I ate the toast and egg. The coffee didn't tempt me. My face was flushed, and I had a wretched headache. While I ate, I tried to make sense of my dream. It was all bound up with Sappho's theory, of course. I was chasing through the shadowed corridors of time after the truth about Vanejul. The other voice was Sappho's, and perhaps the third austere voice from above was common sense, or my conscience warning me away from these otherworldly doings.

What I could not fathom was Vanejul's ambiguous behavior. Was he urging me on, or was he trying to escape? I wished he would come to me again. Then I would know what he wanted.

What *he* wanted? Surely it was what Arabella wanted that I should care about. That was why I was writing the story. Hers was the hand that guided me. Had I let him into my head, despite Mollie's warning? Worse, had I let him into my heart? I felt such an intense longing to see him, to hear him call me "my pet," in that possessive way.

I dragged myself out of bed, dressed, and went downstairs. The phone rang almost the minute I got down. It was Emily. Clairvoyant or not, she had the knack of calling when I needed her most. I told her about my crazy dream and what I thought it meant.

"It is the voice from above that is more interesting," she said. "Your conscience, of course. You are feeling guilty for dabbling in the unknown. The decision is yours, Belle. If you are uncomfortable with it, then by all means desist, or you'll make yourself ill."

"I can't betray Arabella," I said simply.

"Excellent! Then taking to your bed is only an excuse to delay the inevitable. If you want the truth, ask Vanejul when he comes back."

"If he comes back."

"Oh, I think he'll be back now." Her voice sounded so certain.

I thought he would be back, too. "Thanks, Emily."

"The only thanks I want is for you to carry on with your work."

"I don't seem to have much choice."

Chapter Twelve

Slowly I worked my way back into the mood, and the story. When Mollie called at noon and heard I had recovered, she decided she would return to her own house that night.

"Will you be all right?" she asked, concerned.

"I'll be fine. I have Beezle to protect me."

"I don't mean ordinary intruders. I mean Vanejul."

"That's all right, Mollie. I'm not afraid of a ghost." How I longed to see him!

I made a final dinner to serve Mollie that evening when she came to collect her things. She left right after dinner. I brought Beezle in from the yard for company later on. We were developing a routine; he was outdoors during the day, and in the evening he came inside. I had a strong premonition that Vanejul would come, and I was not disappointed. It was about eleven o'clock. I was in the living room, relaxing after my day's work, when I saw a shimmer in the mirror, and looking to discover its source, I watched as Vanejul materialized.

"Where have you been?" I demanded, like a petulant wife.

He tossed up his hands. "Here, there, around and about. Did you miss me, my pet? Perhaps that's why I have stayed away. Absence, you know, is said to make the heart grow fonder—usually of someone else, in my experience."

"I have been wanting to discuss the book with you," I replied, trying to quell the thrill at hearing that familiar "my pet."

Beezle began growling and circling Vanejul. It is impossible to know what he saw or felt, but something raised his hackles. I watched as Vanejul reached out and stroked him. The growls subsided, and Beezle uttered a low whine of pleasure.

"I have a way with animals," Vanejul said, inordinately pleased with himself. Then he cocked his head boldly and added, "Are you not going to say four-legged animals, Belle, in your missish way? It is unlike you to miss a chance to denigrate me."

It seemed ridiculous to even consider this charmer having to resort to rape. Ladies, I felt sure, fell into his lap. I did want to discover what I could of the past, however, and asked his opinion of William, his rival.

He shrugged. "I disliked him cordially, and was jealous as a green cow of his proximity—physical proximity only—to Arabella. Mentally and emotionally, they were leagues apart. He was a cipher, ruled by his very ambitious father. Why do you ask?"

"Just curious about how things were in the old days, your likes and dislikes."

He gazed deeply into my eyes. "You

119

know what I liked, Belle," he said, in a voice as soft and rich as cream.

A warm flush flowed through me. "I know you liked women. What sort of men friends did you have?"

"Regular men. I was closest to my cousin, Hubert Almquist. Why are we discussing my feelings for men? Is it a circuitous way of inquiring my relationship with women? You don't have to be sly with me, Belle. Give me the questions with no bark on them."

"I want to know, for the book."

"This is beginning to sound like a demmed dull book. Men were fellows to talk to about the government and money and literature and our tailors. And of course, the most interesting thing of all—ladies. I was used to hunt and whore with the McDowall brothers, before I met Arabella. Does it surprise you that I admit it?"

"Your wanton ways are no secret, Vanejul."

A scowl creased his brow. "I wish you would not call me that. As you are commending me for my frankness, let there be no secrets between us. I never was much good at discretion anyhow." He spoke openly of his sins, not boasting, exactly, but not discreetly either.

After a moment, he glanced at the television. "Does that gibbering box not drive you to distraction?"

"Yes, it does." I turned it off.

"One sees them everywhere. I am surprised at the duration of this novelty. They inhibit conversation and encourage people to live vicariously. Life is too short, and too precious, to waste in that fashion."

I wished with all my heart I could offer him a glass of wine. I wished he were real. I wished he could have another life, to undo the ills of the first. I sighed sadly.

"Or to waste in any fashion," he added, with a soft smile of regret.

Beezle began barking, and when I looked at Vanejul again, or where he had been, he was gone. But I felt better for his visit. I knew my writing would be better for it, too.

For the next seven days and nights, Chêne Mow was my world, and I had never known a fuller, brighter, happier one. If London burned to the ground, or hurricanes decimated coastal towns, if monarchs fell and battles raged in that vague place, "the east," what was that to me? I was beyond the touch of contemporary calamities, writing my way toward a personal tragedy that took precedence over all else for me.

Arabella met Raventhorpe at the weir again the next night, and the next. They arranged byzantine plots to meet here and there during the day, as well as at the weir at night. They met while riding in the neighborhood and strolling in town. It was in the village that they saw the little golden locket in a jeweler's window, and Arabella admired it. He bought it that same afternoon and had it inscribed. The next time they met, he gave it to her.

They also met by prearrangement at the homes of mutual friends for tea, at the museum at Lyndhurst, in shops, and so on. But these public meetings were never satisfactory. There were too many people present, and they had to be discreet. They could not say the things they wanted to say. Even intimate looks had to be given slyly.

Rides in the countryside were hardly more private, as Arabella was not allowed out without a groom as companion. The first meeting in the spinney might be put down to accident; after the second one, the groom reported it to Sir Giles, and the rides were forbidden. Indeed any communication with Raventhorpe was heavily frowned upon.

She was desolate to think of Raventhorpe waiting for her in the spinney, fearing she stayed away on purpose. She smuggled a note off to him, suggesting he leave a reply in the blasted bole of an oak tree in the park of Chêne Bay. They were both young enough that the intriguing appealed to their romantical natures, and lent the charm of danger and urgency to the affair. Raventhorpe himself was only twenty-one.

At their next meeting, she announced with some relish that she was forbidden to ever see him again.

"There is nothing else for it, I shall beard the lion in his den—call on Sir Giles and ask for permission to court you in the proper manner, with a view to marriage," Raventhorpe declared with commendable promptness.

They were at the weir once more. Their meeting place was an arbor formed by the drooping branches of an old willow. It was exceedingly private, for though autumn was closing in, the willow was still in full leaf. The chilly breeze made an excuse for him to protect her in the warmth of his arms.

Arabella smiled proprietarily, pleased with him, and her own powers, and with life in general. It was no mean accomplishment to have brought this dashing buck to heel.

"That might be best," she concurred.

"And if he refuses—as he undoubtedly will—then what? Will you be a good little girl and do as your guardian commands? Will you stop meeting me?" The words suggested a vulnerability he was far from feeling. He gazed down at her as he spoke, twining a golden curl around his finger. With her bedazzled eyes on him, he had no fear of losing her.

"How can he refuse?" she parried. "You're eligible—the most eligible gentleman in the parish. Your family is good. Better than mine, come to that. I shall be a baroness. He can have nothing against the match except my youth."

"Aye, you've hit it on the head. That is the excuse he'll use."

"Will you wait for me? Wait until my next birthday? Mama married at sixteen, so he cannot set a later date than that."

He pressed her fingers to his warm lips. "I'll wait until the moon turns blue, till the well runs dry, and the cows come home—but I shall wait most impatiently. You mustn't stop seeing me, Belle darling. I need to see you from time to time, to know all is well between us. I'm new at this game of constancy, you must know. I haven't looked at another girl since meeting you."

"You only met me in the spring!" she exclaimed.

"A whole season ago! That is an eternity when you're mad with love. 'Time goes on crutches, till love has all his rites.' Isn't Shakespeare marvelous? He provides a quotation for every occasion." He peered down at her. "You don't even know what I'm talking about, do you, my dear?"

"Of course I do," she said with a missish look. "I've seen the horses do it."

A bark of laughter rang out. "Good God! That puts me in my place! You think me a stallion in rut. Don't think of it like that. It is more than a physical attraction. I think of it as a sacrament between a man and a woman."

She cast a jealous look at him. "How many times have you committed this sacrament, Alexander?"

"Once more, I revert to the Bard. 'What's past is prologue.' From henceforth, you are my only partner in committing that particular sacrament."

"I had better be. Because if I hear of you carrying on with anyone else, I'll marry William to spite you."

"You'd do it, too, minx," he laughed, chucking her chin. "I shall take good care you don't hear of it."

"The only way to be sure I don't hear of it is by your not doing it."

"That is what I meant! What a suspicious little thing you are."

They laughed and talked and flirted, and shared a few innocent kisses that were an entirely novel experience for Arabella, and extremely unsatisfying for Raventhorpe.

Chapter Thirteen

Lord Raventhorpe paid the formal visit to Sir Giles in his study at Chêne Bay, and heard exactly what he expected to hear. Sir Giles pokered up and adopted a righteous tone. The oak-lined office and the handsome desk lent him an air of authority he had not enjoyed before garnering the plum position as Arabella's guardian. In fact, his reputation had been on the shady side. Raventhorpe bristled at the hypocrisy of this parvenu reading him a lecture on morals.

"Arabella is much too young, milord. No offense intended, but your lordship's reputation is not all one could wish in a companion for such a young girl, with no knowledge of the world. In another year, perhaps, we shall see. I had thought of presenting her in London."

Beneath the polite words, the air crackled with suppressed hostility. Their eyes met and held. Raventhorpe's knowing gaze caused a flush to darken Throckley's cheeks.

"Am I to understand you are not allowing anyone to court Arabella for the next year?" he asked.

"She will attend the balls and assemblies, properly chaperoned. Private outings will be curtailed. I do not approve of her slipping off into the park for clandestine meetings."

"That was the only sort of meeting allowed us under your stringent guardianship. I daresay her private meetings will be limited to William?"

Sir Giles bridled up like an angry mare. "What are you suggesting, sir?"

"I am suggesting you would be very happy to see your son marry Arabella's fortune," Raventhorpe answered bluntly. "You shall hear from me if you try forcing her hand."

Throckley reined in his temper. "No one is forcing her to do anything. She is only a child. It is my duty to look out for her best interests. I am extremely busy. I must ask you to leave now, milord."

"It will be my pleasure," Raventhorpe replied, and strode from the room.

He continued meeting Arabella by the weir, but it was a great drain on his time and patience and integrity. The distance of ten miles each way was an obstacle, and as autumn advanced into winter, the weir was no longer a feasible trysting spot. Raventhorpe, accustomed to having things very much his own way, thought Arabella did not appreciate the effort he was making to see her, and his great control in not seducing her. He hinted at the former.

"It's not easy for me either, Alexander," she scolded, shivering as the chilly blast of a November wind invaded her pelisse. "I had to claim a headache to leave Mrs. Melton's dinner party just to be here in time to meet you, and now all you do is scold. It was bad enough that Mrs. Meyers made me take a blue pill to fight off a cold," she said childishly. "And there was to be dancing after dinner at the Meltons' for the youngsters, too."

"I daresay William was of the party?"

"Naturally she invited us all."

"Did William bring you home?"

"Yes. Sir Giles wanted a game of whist. I offered to go home alone. No harm would have come to me with John Groom driving the carriage. I told William to stay for the dancing, but he insisted on coming with me. He is very thoughtful that way."

"Did he take any liberties?"

"William?" she asked, astonished. "Of course not. He's a tame man in a carriage. Tame as a rabbit."

"We all know what rabbits are about, despite their timidity. We can't go on like this, Belle. Throckley's intention is as plain as a pikestaff. He means for you to marry William. If he cannot accomplish it be fair means, he'll do it by foul."

"William would never do anything to harm me! He's like a brother to me."

"He'll do what his father tells him. All it would take is for you to be caught in a compromising situation. They'll press a marriage on you, for the sake of your reputation. If that carriage had broken down, for instance, and you were obliged to spend the night with him..."

"I still wouldn't marry him." She gave a saucy smile, sure of her feminine powers now. "If I'm compromised, I'll marry you instead."

"Generous of you to promise me another man's leavings! Why wait to be compromised? Let's get married now. We'll run away to Gretna Green and be married over the anvil. We could be man and wife. I want you, Belle," he said in a husky voice, as his lips nuzzled the creamy softness of her throat. His arms pulled her against him. When she seemed happy with that, he began stroking her breasts. It was the first time he had done so, and he expected a reprimand.

She didn't say anything, because she was enjoying the unusual sensation. "I want you so much, Belle," he said. He backed her against the bole of the willow tree, with the branches forming a curtain around them. When he leaned against her and pressed his hips to hers, she felt something stir between them, and became frightened. A strange heat flamed in her. "Stop it, Alexander," she said.

"Marry me, Belle," he said in a ragged voice. His fingers began massaging her breasts in a sensual, hypnotic way. She felt her breaths coming in short gasps. Then he began to move his hips against hers, until she felt all hot and dizzy, and more delirious than frightened.

"A runaway match?" she whispered in a breathless voice, half-thrilled and half-outraged.

"Oh God, if I don't have you soon, I'll go mad."

She heard the deep longing in his voice, and felt an exultation of triumph. She slipped away from him, laughing. "Gretna Green is horrid, Alexander. If you really loved me, you wouldn't even suggest it. We'd be ostracized from society. Mrs. Meyers says no one but commoners and hurly-burly girls do that."

Attuned to her every mood, he read the triumph in her tones and stiffened to anger. Why was he letting this chit make a fool of him? "You refuse to marry me, then?" he asked, frowning in displeasure.

"I refuse to make a runaway match with you or anyone else."

"If that's the way you feel, then I am wasting my time riding over here in the cold and damp three times a week."

"It's every bit as cold and damp for me!"

"Then I shan't detain you. And I shan't put you to the great inconvenience of darting from your warm bedchamber a few yards across the park to meet me again."

She stood arms akimbo, glowering at him. "What are you saying, Alexander? That you don't love me? Is it all over, then?"

"I shall leave for London tomorrow. Mama has asked me to accompany her. It was my intention to return almost immediately, but as our meetings have become distasteful to you, I shall stay awhile."

Arabella felt a stab of fear. "I didn't say they were distasteful to me. I would not come if I didn't want to. You just want to go on the strut in London, and are trying to put it in my dish. You'll be out chasing all the girls. I know you."

"That was the old Raventhorpe. I am marble-constant now, but if I go on seeing you, Belle, something will happen. Even marble can take only so much strain before breaking. I am not so domesticated as William."

"So you're really leaving me?" she asked, anger rising.

"For your own good. I shall be back in the spring to reclaim you. Or perhaps earlier—a visit for Christmas. I daresay Sir Giles will take you to the Christmas assembly. He can hardly refuse to let you stand up with me in a public place."

Her heart pinched in fear. "If you leave

now, don't expect me to be waiting for you when you come back. I'm not a book you can put down and pick up when you feel like it."

"Much as I love reading, I have yet to drive twenty miles in a howling wind for the sake of a book."

She resorted to her last weapon in an effort to change his mind, knowing he was fiercely jealous of William. "William never treats me so cavalierly."

"He sounds as if he would make a very good husband for some Bath miss. Good night, Arabella."

"If you leave now, Alexander, I won't be here when you come back. I'll marry William. I will."

"No, you won't. You'll not be satisfied with that man-milliner after knowing me," he said cockily. "*Au revoir*, Belle. That doesn't mean good-bye."

"Yes, it does. I told you, I'll not wait for you, and I won't."

"Suit yourself." He bowed and stalked off to the farther reaches of the park where his mount was tethered.

Before he had ridden a mile, he regretted his rash words, but pride and anger kept him from returning. He had offered to marry her. What more did she want? A runaway match was no less degrading for him than for her, but it was the only marriage open to them. And if they kept meeting, the outcome would be even more degrading. A forced wedding, with a pregnant bride. He could hardly control himself tonight. If Arabella had not brought it to a stop—and even she did not really want to—there was not much doubt how it would have ended.

No, he would not dishonor Arabella or himself by such low behavior. He was still a gentleman after all. Throckley had refused him permission to even call, much less to marry Arabella. If she truly loved him, she would have agreed to go to Gretna Green.

Arabella was equally adamant, and equally angry. Alexander was bored with her. Cuddling and kissing weren't enough to satisfy him. Oh, but it was so lovely tonight, when he held her breasts in the palms of his hands and said in that choking way that he wanted her. She had felt, for those few moments, that she could do anything she wanted with him, and then he had turned into a poker, before her very eyes.

She shook the memory away. He had invented this quarrel for an excuse to go to London and carry on with the debs and lightskirts. That's all it was. She was better of without him. He'd make a terrible husband. She'd never know what he was up to when he was away from her. As the days passed and no word came from him, her anger hardened. She read the local journal, and discovered that he had gone to London. Why should she sit on her thumbs when she knew perfectly well he was carrying on with lightskirts?

Under the approving eye of her guardian, she gave some halfhearted encouragement to William. He was not slow to push his suit forward, but she knew she cared for him no more than she cared for her spaniel.

She allowed him to kiss her once, so she could boast of it later to Raventhorpe. In her heart she knew he would be back. Every day she expected to hear of his return. Kissing William was like kissing a statue. He hardly seemed to know what to do with his lips, and did nothing with his arms except let them hang slack by his sides. If he were Alexander, he would have crushed her against his chest until the air was forced out of her lungs, and her heart felt as if it had leapt up to her throat. His flaming lips would make ruthless demands of hers. William was not so much kissing her as allowing her to kiss him. After two attempts, she gave it up, and William did not institute any lovemaking on his own.

That autumn and winter seemed to drag on endlessly for them both. Raventhorpe did indeed try to amuse himself in the ways Arabella feared, but he found no solace in his former pursuits. The debs seemed like vacuous prudes, and the lightskirts were—lightskirts. The more one paid, the more eager they were to please. It might ease the sexual itch, but what had that to do with love? He wanted Arabella, but he dared not go back to her until they could marry.

In the end, he found solace in pouring out his misery in poetry. It was at that time that he penned his youthful love sonnets, which gave him his first taste of literary fame. Half-ashamed of vaunting his aching heart, he had them published anonymously. John Murray brought them out at the beginning of the year. Raventhorpe remained in town to oversee the proofs during the Christmas holiday. To his astonishment, they were an enormous hit. All of London was seeking to discover their author.

"It wouldn't do the sale any harm to advertise they were written by an eligible and handsome young nobleman," Murray said, peering to assess the poet's mood.

"No point hiding my light under a thimble, eh?" Raventhorpe laughed. "I don't know that I want my name on them, but if you care to whisper the secret in a few select ears, it won't be a secret long."

"Shall I whisper the lady's name as well?" Murray ventured.

Raventhorpe's face closed up like a door. "I think not, Mr. Murray." Then he relaxed into a smile. "A little mystery is a wondrous thing. The lady is not known in London. Her name would add no éclat to the verses. Let her rest in peaceful anonymity."

"A married woman," Murray said to himself, and let the matter drop. But he whispered the secret to Lady Melbourne and Lady Jersey, commonly known as

Silence Jersey, in honor of her unflagging tongue, and before long it was the best-known secret in all of London. Everyone was whispering it. Raventhorpe was famous. His cartoon was seen in store windows, mooning over a lady with a question mark for a face. The chef at the Pulteney Hotel named a raised pie after him; the Prince Regent invited him to an extremely tedious musical evening at Carlton House, and Lady Oxford tried, without success, to seduce him. His slender volume, bearing his name in the second edition, sat on every lady's toilet table and on half the sofa tables of polite London. He luxuriated in his unexpected fame, and could not bring himself to leave London.

Arabella would have his sonnets; they would do his courting for him. Naturally she would buy a copy now that it was common knowledge that he was the poet. He smiled to think how the poems would please her vanity. He thought she might manage to get a note to him, complimenting him. It would be easier for her to write than for him. Her mail was very likely scrutinized by Sir Giles, and they had not arranged to use some disinterested third party as a go-between.

He watched the mail eagerly, and was hurt when no billet-doux came. Never mind, she was angry with him, but she would get over it. But as spring approached, Raventhorpe began to wonder at her prolonged silence. He began scanning the betrothal announcements with a fearful eye. Arabella would not wait forever, even for him. William was with her every day, and with Sir Giles there to nudge them on, anything might happen.

The season of rebirth and renewal after the long chill of winter called up memories of those still-cherished trysts with Arabella, and a desire to reprise them. The air grew warm, and the ladies appeared in their new spring finery. The birds and the fruit trees blossoming in the park reminded him of Chêne Bay. As to a willow tree, he could not see one without repining. It was time to reclaim her. It seemed impossible that Sir Giles could refuse him Arabella's hand now, when he was the cynosure of all eyes in fashionable society.

Even if he did refuse, Raventhorpe felt he now had enough prestige to carry off an elopement without any fear of ostracism. Society would hardly expect less from its premier romantic poet. He would compose a hundred or so lines on the adventure for a lark.

Flushed with success and eager to resume his romance, he had a copy of his *Sonnets to a Lady* bound in white leather with gilt lettering, and inscribed it to Arabella. He set out for Chêne Bay with the book in his pocket.

Chapter Fourteen

At Chêne Bay, Arabella waited impatiently for Alexander's return. It was only the thought of his coming back at Christmas that carried her through bleak November and December. She watched the leaves on "their" willow tree fade from green to yellow, then fall and turn to brown. The very heavens seemed to mourn with her. Tears fell from the leaden sky and oozed drearily down her windowpane. Would Christmas never come?

When he came home for Christmas, she would run away to Gretna Green with him, if he still wanted her. But Raventhorpe did not come at Christmas. He did not even smuggle a message to her. All Christmas day she was on tenterhooks. She went often to the window and peered out at the park, hoping to catch a glimpse of him hiding behind a tree. The days were short in early winter; it was dark before dinnertime, and still he had not come. When she went to her bedchamber on Christmas night, she took the idea that he was waiting for her at the weir. She bundled up in her pelisse and went quietly downstairs.

A light snow was falling. It dusted the ground with diamond sparkles and seemed to hang suspended in the air, but it was not enough snow to keep Raventhorpe away.

She stepped carefully, as she had worn her best slippers. Chancing to look behind her, she saw her footprints. Sir Giles would know she had been out! She peered through the park and saw the unmarked snow. There was no need to go farther. He had not come. She took the broom left by the door to wipe off the snow from incoming boots and brushed out her footprints, then went back to her room. Her heart felt as cold as the snow that covered the land.

Later, rumors of Raventhorpe's growing fame trickled to Chêne Bay, to destroy the last of her hope. In his newfound fame and glory, he had forgotten all about her. Sir Giles, who was interested in politics and subscribed to the London journals, was at pains to keep Arabella informed of Raventhorpe's social progress and to paint it in the deepest hues of lechery. He took the precaution of forbidding to have the book of poems in the house as unfit for decent company. As Arabella was never allowed into Lyndhurst without Mrs. Meyers, this was easily achieved.

"I am glad you turned the fellow off," Sir Giles said, peering at Arabella to see her reaction. He knew of their public meetings and suspected the clandestine ones amounted to more than two meetings in the meadow while riding, but had no positive proof of it. He knew Raventhorpe had been in London for some months in any case, and only made his gibes to prevent a recrudescence of the infatuation.

"Raventhorpe is a byword for lechery in London with these scandalous rhymes he has written—to a lightskirt, very likely, or why is he ashamed to tell the woman's name? I shan't burden your ears with reports of such licentious drivel, Arabella. No decent lady would have him. Well, he is a limb from the family tree when all is said and done, and the world knows what his father was. Now I read he has been taken up by Prinney's set."

"He was at Carlton House?" Arabella exclaimed, impressed in spite of herself.

Sir Giles was swift to talk it down as no honor. "I read that Raventhorpe was invited to join that rackety crew. He will be right at home there. They are no better than they should be, and a deal worse if a quarter of what one reads about them is true. Mistresses and drunken orgies and gambling for high stakes. The lad will be head over ears in debt before the year is out. What a sad trial he is to his poor mama. I pity the lady who marries him."

This last remark brought Arabella to attention. "Does it say he is betrothed?" she asked in alarm, grabbing for the journal.

"Not in this paper," the wily Sir Giles replied. "I read a mention of it somewhere else."

"Who is she?" Arabella demanded.

"Some noble trollop, who thinks a title puts her above the laws of God and man. Best they stick to their own sort and leave respectable people alone. But what is Raventhorpe to us, eh?" he asked heartily. "The only wedding we are interested in is yours, my dear Arabella. I expect you will be choosing your groom one of these days. You are not far from your sixteenth birthday."

He watched as her pointed little chin quivered, and she struggled to fight back the tears. "Why, my dear, you are not still thinking of that ramshackle lad? I made sure you were over him long ago. He could not wait a year for you—I told him, against my better judgment, to come back when you were sixteen. How long would he have been a faithful husband if he could not wait a year? You know who cares for you more deeply and truly, I think," he said, with a sly glance from the corner of his eyes.

Arabella turned and fled from the room. She did not cry after all; she was beyond tears. She paced her chamber in a fit of fury, tossing obstacles aside and kicking the furniture to vent her wrath. What a fool she had been to think Raventhorpe loved her. He complained at having to ride ten miles to see her. He had darted straight off to London and fallen in love with some grand lady. He need not think she was crying willow for him! If he meant to bring his lady to the neighborhood and lord it over her, he would get his comeuppance. She would marry William, and it would not be an ignominious dart to Scotland to be married over the anvil either. How dare he suggest she make a runaway match to Gretna Green? That should have showed her what kind of man he was.

That evening after dinner she asked to speak to Sir Giles in his study. He was not slow in darting forward to accompany her thither.

Sitting on the very edge of the chair he drew forward for her, she said in a voice bereft of emotion, "I have decided to marry William, if you would like, Uncle Giles."

His fleshy face broke into smiles of delight. "My dear! You have made me the happiest man in England. William will be in raptures."

"He hasn't asked me, actually," she said, in an ironic tone she had never used before, "but I am happy that it pleases you."

"He will ask you this very night; you may be sure of that. I see no point in dallying, now that the matter is settled. Fifteen is a little young, to be sure, but your birthday is fast approaching. What do you say we have the marriage the day after, on June the tenth?"

"Whatever you think best, Uncle. I have only one stipulation." Sir Giles looked at her warily. "I would like a lavish wedding," she said. If Alexander offered her a runaway match, she would show him what other beaux offered.

"Whatever you wish, my dear," he said, stifling a sigh of relief. "We want only your happiness."

"I want the finest wedding the parish has ever seen. We must begin preparations at once."

"I shall speak to Mrs. Meyers within the hour. My dear, what pleasure it will be to hear you call me Papa. You know, I think, it has always been my wish that you and William should marry. What could be more natural, more right? Cousins, friends from the egg, both of good character. No one in his right mind could say a word against it."

"Why should anyone object?" she asked.

Sir Giles was ambushed by the memory of a pair of steaming black eyes and the insolent speech. *I am suggesting you would be very happy to see your son marry Arabella's fortune. You shall hear from me if you try forcing her hand.* But he was not forcing her. She had suggested it herself. She would be sixteen before the marriage took place, the age he had mentioned as being eligible.

Sir Giles had an unfortunate combination of cowardice, greed, and hypocrisy in his makeup. Had he been less a coward, he would have stolen Arabella's fortune by some financial chicanery or forced her to marry his son. If he had been less greedy, he would not have coveted her money. But he wanted it all—his good reputation, her money, and no trouble. It seemed now he had accomplished his aim. William was a biddable fellow. He would do as his father said, about both the girl and the money.

"Object? Why, no one in his right mind would object," he repeated.

Arabella left in a shower of good wishes and compliments that she ignored completely. Her only pleasure in the betrothal was the pain it would cause Alexander. William was called in and told he was to marry Arabella.

"Did she agree?" he asked doubtfully.

Sir Giles was too well pleased to give voice to any of the sarcastic speeches that sprang to mind. "Certainly she agreed. She is eager to have you. June the tenth is to be the day. You may plan a wedding trip, William. The Lake District or Scotland, whatever she likes."

"Very well, Papa."

Next it was Mrs. Meyers, who was called in and told to begin the wedding preparations. This dame was less easily convinced of Arabella's willingness. Uncertain what she should do, she had discovered the nocturnal visits to the weir and scolded Arabella, but she had not told Sir Giles. There was more romance in her than Arabella suspected. She had watched her charge's summer blossoming and her winter's decline with worried eyes. When she went to Arabella's room to discuss the wedding plans, her charge assured her there was no undue persuasion being used.

"It is my own decision," Arabella said stiffly. "I only hope William does not dislike it too much."

"What is to dislike? He would look long

143

and far before finding another such heiress to have him. Dislike it indeed!" She noticed the pillows and books tossed about the room and began picking them up.

A frown settled on her kindly face. "Arabella, this hasn't anything to do with Raventhorpe, has it?"

"What is he to me?" her charge replied with a toss of her curls. "I haven't given Raventhorpe a thought since he went to London and turned poet. Next month I shall be sixteen, the age at which my mama married. I have a mind to be getting on with my life, and William will make an unexceptionable husband. Let us discuss my gown, Mrs. Meyers. I want white satin, or do you think lace more dashing?"

Arabella displayed a keen interest in the wedding, but Mrs. Meyers, who had known her for years, sensed the anger and hurt below the surface. It seemed it was not a marriage she wanted, but a lavish wedding. Mrs. Meyers made a few more queries, but they were brushed aside peremptorily. Arabella was growing up. She no longer wanted to be petted and pampered, and spill out her little hurts to her old friend. There was deep hurt there, but with luck, a good marriage would heal it. There would be children soon, and the busy life of a matron. William would make a good, steady husband. Lord, it was enough to make a cat laugh, to think of little Belle being Mrs. Throckley, and calling on other matrons. It made one feel old.

Sir Giles wasted no time in sending the wedding notice to the local papers. He had William drive Arabella around to call on neighbors and go into Lyndhurst with her by his side, to show the world how happy she was. Her happiness took the form of eagerly scanning the streets for a glimpse of Alexander. A dozen times she saw a blue jacket and a curled beaver that looked exactly like his. But when the carriage drew closer, she noticed the shoulders were not quite as broad, or the walk was flat-footed, or some other imperfection was there.

When the spring assembly was announced, Sir Giles insisted she and William attend. They would all go together, one happy family. Strangely, Arabella showed very little interest, after having had a new gown made up, and insisting on attending a series of waltzing lessons in Lyndhurst.

It was on one of her trips to Lyndhurst with William that she saw a copy of the *Sonnets to a Lady* in the everything shop and bought it while William perused the fish lures. She slipped it into her reticule without saying a word. That night she read it in bed, and knew before she had read three poems that she was the lady of the sonnets. There was not a single doubt in her mind. The clandestine meetings, the stolen kisses, even the rides in the dark to the weir, though he called it a lake—they were all there, transmuted by the magic of poetry into an ideal of young love.

How had it gone wrong? Her first wave of regret soon faded to pique. He had used their love to make himself famous. For her, it had been a private, secret pleasure, but he had torn even the consolation of her memories from her by shouting them to the world. Serving wenches and courtesans were smirking over the words he had said to her. Yes, he even used some of the same phrases he had whispered in her ear, making her blush for joy. She felt soiled and degraded to know she was now public property, and thanked providence that no one knew who the lady was. Perversely, his secrecy rankled, too. He was ashamed to tell the world he had loved her.

As the days wore on, Arabella began to hatch a plan of revenge on Raventhorpe. It began as no more than a means of alleviating the pain when she lay in bed at night, remembering their past and trying to sleep. She would picture meeting Raventhorpe, she all grown-up into a fine lady, and with a wedding ring on her finger. The scales would fall from his eyes; he would at last come to realize he had lost the only lady he could ever love. As Raventhorpe was in London and apparently planned to stay there, her daydreams shifted themselves to that city.

As her dissatisfaction grew, she began to think she might make the dream a reality. She and William would hire a house in London and stay for a year. Why return before next spring? Winter at Chêne Bay was a gray, dreary season. And best of all, they would be away from Sir Giles. Her guardian was kindness itself, and she felt guilty for wanting to escape him. She told herself it would hardly seem like being married at all to stay in the same house with him and Mrs. Meyers, for she could not like to dismiss her old companion.

She mentioned the extended London visit to William, who took the plan to his father. That gentleman was too wily to scotch the plan before the wedding. He would allow them a honeymoon visit to the city, as Arabella expressed no interest in the Lake District or Scotland. Two or three weeks, there could be no harm in that, when she had the wedding ring on her finger.

The approaching wedding gave Arabella little joy, but it gave her activity at least, and prevented her from moping. She amused herself by amassing a trousseau elegant enough to set London on its ear, but even a closetful of lovely gowns and dashing bonnets and shawls and gloves did not fill the ache in her heart.

Sir Giles smiled benignly at her fussing over silks and bonnets and gloves. Let her drape herself in all the latest fashions. The quizzes could not say he was depriving her of her fortune, and the cost was small enough after all. But when she began to speak of hiring a house and staying in London for a year, he put his foot down.

"You forget you have an estate to run,

my dear. Chêne Bay does not take care of itself."

"You have always run the estate for me, Uncle."

"It has been my pleasure to give you a hand while you were young, but how are we to make a businessman of William if he is off gallivanting in London? Marriage imposes duties as well as pleasures, Arabella. Then, too, there is your nursery to consider," he said archly. "A healthy young bride like you, it is fourpence to a groat you will be enceinte before the summer is over. That is no time to be gallivanting. You will find two weeks in London more than enough to enjoy the theaters and drives and shops. One tires of London after a short while. I shall write to a hotel and arrange rooms. No point hiring a house for two weeks."

She appealed to William, who repeated his father's excuses almost verbatim. And she was powerless to force the issue. Sir Giles was her guardian. Once she married William, he would be her lord and master—and banker. She grew restless and cross. It was her money; why must she do as they said? If marriage was to give her no independence, what was the point of it? She did not love William. She was frightened to death to think of having babies. She would sink into an old housewife without ever having enjoyed her youth.

That was her mood when she went to the spring assembly and met Raventhorpe once more.

Chapter Fifteen

Arabella's hair, arranged high on her head in the new style she had adopted since her betrothal, added an air of sophistication to her youthful charms. Amidst her golden curls she placed the pearl combs William had given her for an engagement present. Now that she was engaged, she could put off the modest white gowns of youth. She wore a blue shot silk, cut daringly low at the bodice. Mrs. Meyers squinted at the incipient swell of white bosoms, but did not give verbal vent to her displeasure. That battle had been waged between them, and lost by the companion.

"I am no longer a child," Arabella had said, with a toss of her impertinent little shoulders. But really she still looked remarkably like a child dressed up in her mama's clothes.

When Raventhorpe spotted her across the room at the assembly, he scarcely recognized her. He had left a pretty, charming young hoyden, and came back to find her changed into a beautiful, poised lady. He was intrigued by the look of hauteur and ennui on her young face. A maiden should not assume the world-weary expression of a dowager, and yet there was charm in the impersonation. Her eyes, especially, looked as if she had experienced all of life, but most particularly its sorrows.

He gazed, mesmerized by the change in her. Not lacking in vanity, he ascribed her boredom to the weariness of life without him, and looked forward to seeing it dissipate when she caught her first glimpse of him. Then their eyes met for a brief moment, and her ennui hardened to iron. The vixen was feigning indifference to repay him for his long absence.

She looked away quickly, hoping no one could hear the banging of her heart, or feel the heat of the fire that raged within her. She turned to flee, and felt the steely grip of Sir Giles on her elbow.

He knew he must confront Raventhorpe eventually. He preferred to do it in a public place, where violence might be controlled by concern for propriety.

"I believe your old friend Raventhorpe is trying to catch your eye, my dear," he said. "He will want to stand up with you. Might as well get it over with, eh? One dance can do no harm."

Even as he spoke, Raventhorpe was pacing rapidly forward, his wicked black eyes devouring Arabella, while a smile of anticipation lifted the corners of his lips. Towering in the confidence of his literary success, he felt sure of his welcome. He made his bows first to Arabella, then turned a cool expression on her guardian.

"Sir Giles," is all he said.

Sir Giles returned the bow with an equally curt "Milord," delivered in the stiff tones of animosity performing its public duty.

Raventhorpe turned again to the lady and made a leisurely examination of her from head to foot, with always that little smile resting on his lips. When he spoke, his voice was husky with emotion. "Arabella, how charming you look this evening. May I have the next dance?"

Arabella's tongue cleaved to the roof of her mouth. She just looked, as if seeing a devil. It was Sir Giles who answered. "She will be happy to stand up with you, milord. We have all heard of your fame in London. I do not go in for poetry reading myself, but my friends assure me your works are something out of the ordinary," he said, with that faint praise that sets a narrow limit on approval.

The words were not hostile, which led Raventhorpe to believe Sir Giles had accepted the inevitable and was giving him permission to court Arabella.

"Thank you, Sir Giles," he replied.

Taking Arabella's cold hand, he placed it on his sleeve and walked her away. The susurration of her silken skirt was the only sound as they left. Despite the tumult of words reeling in her head, Arabella could not trust herself to speak, and Raventhorpe seemed content just to look down at her, with pleasure beaming in his eyes.

When the music began, she went like one in a trance to join the dancers. "Ah, a waltz," he said. "Has this devil's dance made its way to the depths of the New Forest yet?"

"Yes, I have taken lessons," she said quietly. She had been envisaging Raventhorpe as a depraved lecher, but upon seeing him again close at hand, seeing his youthful vigor and the old love shining in his eyes, her heart wavered, and was soon recaptured.

He drew her into his arms, and for a few bars they waltzed without speaking. Their bodies swayed lightly in harmony with the music, and with each other. For Arabella, it was like having found the other half of herself. That aching void that yawned inside her was gone, filled with a trembling pleasure that was more than half exquisite pain. She felt hot tears rising, and blinked them away.

"I've missed you so much, Belle," he said, gazing softly at her. "If it weren't for reliving our moments together in my poetry, I think I would have gone mad. I've had a copy of the verses bound specially in white kid for you, with gold embossing. Did you like the sonnets?"

What had she done? What utter folly had she committed? "They were lovely, Alexander," she managed to murmur.

"I wanted to shout from the rooftops who was their inspiration. Until we are married, that might be a tad indiscreet, but when you are Lady Raventhorpe, prepare to find yourself an object of—"

"Stop it!" A sob caught in her throat.

"There now, I know exactly how you feel, my love," he said softly. "It's a demmed bore, having to be with a crowd when we want to be alone, but we shall meet once more at the weir tonight for old times' sake."

She just looked, with tears gathering in her eyes while her lips trembled uncertainly. Raventhorpe thought she was overwhelmed with joy, as he was himself. His arms tightened instinctively around her. He knew she was on the point of tears and tried to lighten the mood.

"Well, my darling, you've grown up most delightfully while I have been away. Soon you will be sweet sixteen, and Sir Giles will have no excuse to refuse us permission to marry. It has been the longest winter of my—"

"I am engaged to William," she said in a flat voice. "We plan to marry on the tenth of June."

Raventhorpe stopped dead in his tracks. He looked at her in bewilderment. A few heads turned to stare at the young couple, standing motionless on the dance floor.

"You're joking, of course," he said. "That's a nasty stunt, Belle. You demmed near gave me a heart attack. Fair enough, you deserve one kick at the cat for my not being in touch with you, but—"

"People are staring at us, Alexander," she hissed.

He seized her hand in a crippling grip and led her at a quick pace from the floor into the refreshment parlor, which was nearly empty so early in the evening. "I'd like to keep on walking, right out the door so we could be alone," he said. "I want to kiss you to death. Shall we?" A reckless grin lifted his lips and lit his dark eyes.

Gazing at her, Raventhorpe saw the tension in her body and the misery on her pale face, and knew she was serious. Her lips worked silently in a futile effort to speak. His strong hands gripped her arms. "Belle, what is it?" he demanded. "Are you really engaged? Did that bastard force you—" Beyond speech, she only shook her head. His eyes glittered like black diamonds in the pale mask of his face. "What are you saying, my dear? Tell me. I don't understand."

She found strength then to tell him. The months of agony had their brief, bitter revenge. Pride lent a harsh edge to her voice as she said, "I'm marrying William. What's so hard to understand about that? I told you I would. You left me all alone for months on end. Never a visit, never a word." Her voice rose to the edge of hysteria.

"The hell you are!" he growled.

"I am." She lifted her left hand and showed him the circlet of baguette diamonds William had given her. "It's all settled," she said, tossing her chin in the air. "There's nothing you can do about it, so you might as well go and leave us in peace."

Raventhorpe willed down a howl of rage. When he spoke, he tried for an air of indifference, but she heard the hurt below it, and wanted to throw herself into his arms. "Is that what you want, then? You are doing this freely, of your own choice?" he asked.

"No one is forcing me."

"Then there's nothing more to say. I shall return to London at once."

Her lips flew open, and a look of utter despair showed on her face. "Oh, Alexander, you must help me! I've done something dreadful. I thought you had forgotten all about me."

"Forgotten you? I have been waiting an eternity for you to turn sixteen. I didn't trust myself to go on meeting you alone. It seemed best to stay away until we could marry."

Sir Giles, worried to know they were alone, appeared at the doorway. "Has Belle told you the news? She has accepted William's offer," he said, advancing timorously. He read the danger in Raventhorpe's glare, and stopped a few feet from him. Over the punch bowl he continued, "Arabella was in a hurry to get the thing done. No point in waiting, eh?"

"I am sure *Arabella* was in a great hurry to marry your son," Raventhorpe sneered.

Seeing Raventhorpe's mood and knowing his reckless nature, Arabella was at pains to avert disaster. "I have told Raventhorpe all about it, Uncle," she said. "He understands the matter."

"That it was your own idea?" Sir Giles asked.

She did not confirm or deny it verbally, but just nodded her sullen agreement.

"May I wish you happy, Belle," Raventhorpe said through clenched jaws. "This will be a lesson to me. Next time I fall in love, I shan't be put off. If you will both pardon me now, I shall retire to some quiet waterfall and compose a few lines on my broken heart. Good night, Sir Giles." He turned to Belle, with a meaningful look. "Belle—good-bye, my dear. I wish you every joy."

He bowed, turned, and strode from the room. Sir Giles breathed a great sigh of relief. That hadn't gone so badly as he feared. Raventhorpe had only been amusing himself with Arabella, as he thought all along. He took Belle's arm and said, "Let us return to the dance, my dear. William will be wondering what has happened to you."

It was always Sir Giles who did William's courting for him. When he delivered Belle back to her fiancé, she seemed to be in fair spirits. In truth, she was hardly aware that she was at an assembly at all. In her heart Raventhorpe's words echoed, *I shall retire to some quiet waterfall.* He was telling her he would meet her at the weir, and he would somehow straighten out this impossible mess. Because he still loved her. He had always loved her. And she loved him so much, she felt brittle all over to think of it. It seemed her flesh had turned to crystal, which might be shattered at a touch, unleashing all the passion pent up in her.

She danced with half a dozen gentlemen without seeing or hearing them. At supper she sat guarded on one side by William, on the other by Sir Giles. She ate her favorite lobster patties and cream tarts and drank wine. But in her mind, she was with Alexander at the weir. A newly engaged lady was allowed to enjoy a state of distraction, and her friends smiled tolerantly amongst themselves.

After the assembly, she went to her bedroom and waited until the house fell silent. It was two o'clock before she felt safe to slip downstairs and out the library door, which was the least likely to be overheard. The friendly night was warm as she skimmed through the shadows, down the incline to the water, whose black depths sparkled silver and gold on the surface from the moonlight's reflection.

In the distance she saw a tall, broad-shouldered silhouette etched in charcoal against the silver sky, and hastened forward. Raventhorpe was waiting, as she knew he would be. He turned at her approach, held his arms open, and she flew into them. He crushed her against him and lifted her off the ground, while he kissed her with thundering passion. His lips moved possessively over her eyes, slid down her cheek to her throat, where she felt a moist warmth touch her; all the while his arms bound her to him with violent force. Between kisses, he rained a breathless shower of sweet love words into her ears.

"My darling, it's been so long. Many a night I ached to be with you, to see your sweet face, to feel you. I thought the time would never come. Nothing will ever keep us apart again. Nothing. I couldn't bear it. This is all my fault. I should not have left you alone. I thought you knew how much I loved you. I thought the poems would reassure you. I put my heart and soul into them."

She soaked up the words like a parched flower devouring water. A vital force spread through her body, enlivening it. "They're beautiful, Alexander," she murmured. Her fingers moved lightly over his face, as if testing to be sure he was real. "I knew they were about us."

He stepped back and frowned at her. "Then why did you do this appalling thing? Was it only to bring me back? Surely you knew I would come."

"I didn't know it. How could I? I thought you'd forgotten all about me. Oh, Alexander, you don't know how I've suffered, thinking you were with other women. Sir Giles told me you were going to marry a great lady."

"And so I am. You."

"What did I care who I married if I couldn't marry you? Maybe I did hope you'd hear and come to put a stop to it. I never meant to do it up so soon. This was Uncle Giles's idea. And he won't let me go to London either, except for a measly two weeks. I wanted to live there a year, so you'd see me in my new finery and wearing a golden band. Then you'd be sorry you'd lost me."

A reluctant smile tugged at his lips, to hear that beneath the new veneer of sophistication, she was still the same impulsive, childish, vain, adorable Arabella.

"So what is to be done?" he said.

"We'll have to tell Sir Giles."

"Surely it is William who is more concerned?"

"No. He just does what Uncle Giles tells him. I don't think he even loves me. At least that's in our favor. I mean his heart won't be broken. I shouldn't like to hurt poor William."

"I shall call on Sir Giles tomorrow. It may get nasty. No need for you to see us lashing our tails and snarling at each other. The thing to do is pack up a bag and be ready to go to Oldstead Abbey. You can stay with Mama until we arrange a wedding."

She looped her arms around his neck and laid her head on his chest. His hand cupped the nape of her neck, enjoying the warmth of her. "Are we really going to be married, then?" she said dreamily. "I can hardly believe it."

"Nothing will stop us. I don't give a tinker's curse if I have to put a bullet through the pair of them."

She raised her head and scowled at him. "Don't talk like that, Alexander. You frighten me."

"You frighten too easily," he laughed. "That is why I don't want you present for the interview. If Sir Giles refuses to let me see you, I'll storm up the stairs and carry you away by main force. Be prepared to flee."

"I shall pack tonight. I don't want to leave all my trousseau behind. I've got half a dozen new gowns and bonnets, Alexander, of the very latest style. I'll do you proud in London. You won't have to be ashamed of me in front of your fine friends."

He chucked her chin. "Vain creature, worrying about gowns at a time like this. You are all I want."

She basked in the luxury of his love. "I want you to be proud of me when we go to London."

"I should always be proud of you, even if you were in rags."

He drew forth the copy of his sonnets, bound in white kidskin, and gave it to her. "I had this made up especially for you. If I ever have to leave you again for any reason, I want you to read it from time to time, just to remind you how much I love you."

"I'll always treasure it," she said, "but you mustn't leave me again. I was sorry I'd refused to go to Gretna Green with you. I don't care if you go to America, or Africa, or off to war in Spain. I'll put on trousers and go with you."

"You would, too, minx."

In a reckless mood, Raventhorpe accompanied Belle to the library door and kissed her good night, with long, sweetly lingering kisses. It was hard to control his passion when she clung so desperately to him, as if she feared to let him go. Tenderness and love held his desire in check, and he detached her arms reluctantly. There was time for that. He could wait. When he left, he was whistling softly.

Chapter Sixteen

Sir Giles, leery of Raventhorpe's easy capitulation, was brooding in his study. He did not see Belle and Raventhorpe together, but he heard that insouciant whistle, and recognized the pair of shoulders strutting boldly through the park. He feared he had not heard the last of Raventhorpe. Sir Giles was awake very late that night, preparing his plan, and was ready for Raventhorpe when he called the next morning, with his impossible demand.

"You are imagining things, milord," Sir Giles said firmly when Raventhorpe charged him with rushing a wedding upon Arabella. The meeting took place at ten o'clock the next morning. Sir Giles stood behind the desk in his study. He always felt safer with a physical barrier between himself and this hotheaded young lord.

"Am I imagining that you have arranged

a wedding the very day after her sixteenth birthday? You were taking no chances! What is the rush?"

"It was Arabella herself who initiated these wedding plans. She is very much in love with William."

"She suggested the match to frighten me. It was yourself who rushed the wedding forward with such unseemly haste. I tell you she is in love with me, and I with her. I mean to marry her, Sir Giles, with or without your consent," Raventhorpe declared.

"You are a demmed liar! She loves William."

A steely glint gleamed in Raventhorpe's eyes. "Watch what you are about, sir. A gentleman does not take kindly to being called a liar."

"A liar and a rake, preying on an innocent young girl who happens to be under my protection."

Raventhorpe's lips thinned in fury. "You will either retract that charge, or pay dearly for it."

"Name your second, milord. My second will call on him to settle the time and place where we meet."

Raventhorpe could hardly believe the old man had the fortitude to go to this length. He felt a new respect creep in to dilute the contempt he had always felt for Sir Giles. The whole idea of a duel with Arabella's guardian was extremely repugnant to him, but to be called a liar and a rake! The fellow was forcing a duel on him.

"Can't we settle this like gentlemen?" he said reluctantly.

"A gentleman would not fail to accept a challenge," Sir Giles taunted.

"If you insist, let it be on your head. My cousin, Sir Hubert Almquist, will oblige me. William will know where to find him."

Raventhorpe was so upset, he left without speaking to Arabella. It was from Sir Giles that she heard a warped version of the story when he had her summoned to his office later, after he had settled down. Such decisive action was alien to Sir Giles, and at his age his heart did not take kindly to it. It took two glasses of brandy to keep up his courage for the pending trouble.

"Lord Raventhorpe has been to call," he announced sternly. "I was forced into a duel to protect my honor and yours, Arabella."

Her face blanched in horror. "A duel! Uncle, you mustn't think of such a thing."

"After such assaults as he made on my good name, I had no option but to oblige him."

"What did he say?"

"He accused me of forcing you into an unwanted marriage for the sake of your money. I daresay he thinks I have squandered your fortune. I have never taken a sou but what was needed to run your estate and the salary suggested by a disinterested lawyer. Even that, I have set aside, for the most part, for you and William. And for those years of toil and devotion to you, I am forced by that rake to risk my life defending my honor."

"But he'll kill you!"

"I have no doubt that is exactly what he has in mind. He thinks he would have easy work of William once I am gone. It will certainly be the death of me," he said, clutching his heart, "but if it opens your eyes to Raventhorpe's true nature, it will be worth it."

"I cannot believe Alexander has behaved so badly, so foolishly."

"Foolish, is it? He is clever as a serpent. No doubt he has wasted his own fortune on the London lightskirts and wants to get his hands on yours to continue his wanton ways. But we shall defeat him, my dear. The thing to do—you must marry William at once. In that manner, Raventhorpe cannot plunder your fortune."

"Marry William? But—"

"You are engaged to him, after all," Sir Giles said sharply. "You cannot mean to jilt him, to break his heart and make a laughingstock of him in the parish when he would not harm a hair of your head. To put the wedding forward a month can make no difference."

Arabella was in such a state of confusion, she hardly knew what to think, much less what to do. She did not believe Raventhorpe was marrying her for her dowry; this was another of Sir Giles's stunts. But she did not intend to let Raventhorpe kill her uncle either. And it was true William would look foolish when she left him. Oh, it was all such a muddle! She must consult with Alexander before taking any step. She would not make a scene until she had been in touch with him and heard his advice.

"I am afraid I must insist on this, Arabella," Sir Giles continued. "I fear you are not totally innocent in this affair. I know you met Raventhorpe last night after the ball. Don't bother to deny it. I do not blame you; you are young, and no doubt he can turn a girl's head without much trouble. He has had plenty of experience at that game, but it is my duty to protect you. The wedding will take place tomorrow morning, right here at Chêne Bay."

"Tomorrow! No, that is too soon, Uncle. The preparations are not complete."

"You and William can have a wedding party a little later. It is the only way I can be sure Raventhorpe does not run off with your money, for once he has killed me, you will have only William to protect you. He would make short shrift of William, who dislikes violence. You know his peaceful ways."

"Tomorrow," she said pensively. That gave her a day to make other plans.

"Tomorrow morning," Sir Giles added, and stared at her until she felt compelled to obey.

"Very well, Uncle," she said meekly, for she knew she would not leave the room until she had agreed. To resist would only raise his suspicions, and perhaps see her locked in her room.

Belle left the study in a blind panic. She had to stop this duel. Much as she loved Raventhorpe, she sensed that recklessness in him. Had he not made some careless mention of putting a bullet through both Sir Giles and William? This was no way to repay her uncle for his years of selfless devotion. And William for being a harmless pawn. She could never be happy to take a bridegroom with blood on his hands.

She sat alone in her room, gazing with unseeing eyes at the park. She had to stop this duel, but she was unwilling to give up Raventhorpe. What she must do was run away with him before the duel. Yes, that was the best thing. The problem would be to convince Raventhorpe to go along with her. Men had such troublesome notions of honor. She must deliver an ultimatum; tell him she would not marry him if he fought the duel. Her uncle, she thought, would be vastly relieved and happy to accept an apology. And really he deserved one, for he had not forced her to marry William, and had been a conscientious guardian of her monies. Uncle would accept the apology, and the wedding to William need not be rushed forward. Before it took place, she and Alexander would be gone.

Her gowns were already packed. It remained only to get them out of the house to someplace convenient to the main road, where she could transfer them to Raventhorpe's carriage. She thought of Chêne Mow, the little flint cottage at the bottom of the park. It had been standing empty for a month, since the death of the last occupant. It was being spruced up with the intention of hiring it to the local doctor. She would tell the servants she was taking some curtains and linens down to make it more comfortable. And in her note to Raventhorpe she would ask him to meet her there that night. The weir was no longer safe. Sir Giles had tumbled to it.

Timmie McGee, the groom's helper, had delivered notes to Raventhorpe for her in the past. When he came to pick up her gowns, masquerading in hampers as the curtains and linens for Chêne Mow, she gave him the note, and a crown to insure his silence. In the note she told of her uncle's plans for an early wedding, begged Raventhorpe to apologize to Sir Giles, and to meet her at Chêne Mow at midnight. They would go to Oldstead Abbey to be married at once.

She spent a fretful, restless day, hearing Raventhorpe castigated as a villain by Sir Giles and William. A troubled Sir Hubert Almquist came to call and stayed only a moment. Arabella could not discover whether there had been an apology. If so, it had not been accepted. She learned from William of the arrangement as to time and place of the duel. They were to meet in a certain clearing in the spinney at seven the next morning. She had thought William would be his father's second in the duel but learned Mr. Withers, her uncle's friend and solicitor from Lyndhurst, had accepted the office. While Sir Giles and Raventhorpe aimed their pistols at each other, she and William were to be married.

"At seven o'clock in the morning?" she exclaimed, when William brought her this detail.

"Papa is afraid Raventhorpe would get wind of it and make trouble if the vicar came today. He thought it best for the vicar to come while Raventhorpe is at the spinney, you see. Then if he kills Papa, well, at least your fortune is safe. We are already married."

"Don't you mean *I* am safe, William?" she asked coolly.

"Just so, my dear. I am only telling you what Papa said. I wish he had accepted the apology, but really it was the outside of enough, to accuse him of forcing a match on you. It was all your own idea," he added unhappily.

So Raventhorpe had apologized. "It was, and I am sorry I dragged you into it, William, for you don't want me any more than I want you."

"I daresay we shall suit well enough."

The day seemed endless. Sir Giles requested that she not leave the house, no doubt for fear that Raventhorpe was skulking about, ready to steal her away. She went to her room, but even there she found no peace. Mrs. Meyers nearly caught her reading the book of poems Alexander had given her the night before. She quickly stuffed it into the back of the secret drawer in her toilet table. Dinner was a somber affair. Sir Giles attempted a few rallying remarks about this being Arabella's last evening as a "spinster," and she smiled weakly. William drank a good deal of wine, which was unlike him.

Chapter Seventeen

It was just after dinner that Arabella had her reply from Raventhorpe. He wrote:

My own dear Belle:
This is intolerable! Your uncle would not accept an apology. It is clear he wants to kill me by fair means or foul. As to forcing you to marry William! I shall meet you at midnight tonight at Chêne Mow, as you suggest, and take you—and all your new finery—to Oldstead to stay for the nonce. But pray do not ask me to cry craven on the duel. I, and in some collateral way you, would carry the shame of cowardice with us until death. Neither pride nor common sense recommends that course to me. I shall not let Throckley make a William of me.
I shall meet your uncle, but I shall not kill him. A wound, high on the shoulder,

169

will teach him a lesson without putting him in his grave. Almquist is awake on all suits. He will see there is no trickery in the affair. I would give a year of my life to avoid this duel. That is one disgrace I have managed to avoid, until now. Outside of war or some chance heroic deed, there is no honor in killing or being killed. We shall meet at Chêne Mow at midnight, and soon we shall be together for good. Don't, I beg of you, do anything foolish, like confronting Sir Giles on your own. All our future happiness depends on your discretion. All my love, always.

Toujours,
Alexander.

She read it twice, with some satisfaction. Like Alexander, she dreaded the duel, but at least he had promised not to kill Sir Giles. Alexander was a famous shot; she had no doubts of his ability to place a bullet just where he intended. He would meet her at Chêne Mow tonight, and take her to his mama to await the wedding tomorrow. Sir Giles would have too much on his mind in the morning to check her bedroom and see she was not there. He would not learn of her departure until he returned from the duel.

There would be talk and ill feelings and unpleasantness between themselves and Sir Giles for some time to come, but in the end all would smooth itself out. She would make a generous settlement on Sir Giles for all his help over the years. Money was all he really cared about. The important thing was to prevent bloodshed.

She had a wistful memory of the young girl who had been shocked at the thought of a runaway match, but really it would have been less scandalous than a duel. Like father, like son, people would say of Alexander. It never entered her head that anything could go wrong when Raventhorpe was in charge of her rescue. In the noble strength of his gilded youth, he seemed invincible.

She went to her room early that evening, ostensibly to retire and be rested for her early morning wedding. Sir Giles suggested William do the same, and like a sheep, he did as he was told. At eleven-thirty she stole downstairs and listened for sounds of Sir Giles. His study door was open; the study was dark. He was not in the saloon either. She thought perhaps he had slipped away under cover of darkness to make plans with the vicar for the morning. She went into the library and out the French door.

Arabella wore a dark habit to conceal her movements lest anyone should be looking out the window. Fleeing through the shadows, she wondered when she would see her home again. She remembered then that she had left Alexander's letters and her special copy of his poems hidden in her bedroom. With so much preying on her mind, she had forgotten them, but they would be safe there. With Alexander by her side, there was no hurry to regain those tokens.

As she approached Chêne Mow, she saw a light burning in the kitchen, and was surprised that Raventhorpe was there so early. She would scold him for lighting the lamp. It was not likely anyone would see it in this secluded place, but if Sir Giles happened to be returning from his visit to the vicar, he might go to investigate.

She stopped at the window and stood on tiptoe to look in, wanting a glimpse of Alexander, caught unawares. She gave a soft gasp of surprise. It was not Raventhorpe who was there but Sir Giles, and he was not alone. She recognized Bert Robinson, a disreputable poacher and ne'er-do-well from the neighborhood. His father had one of her tenant farms. What were they doing together in this hidden little cottage? She looked again and saw Sir Giles handing Robinson a pistol. Her blood turned to ice at the look of angry determination on her uncle's face. He looked ready to commit murder.

She was consumed with eagerness to hear what they were saying, and crept to the back door. They had left it ajar. It led through a shed to the kitchen. She crept through the dark shed to the inside door, close enough to hear. Through a small opening, she could even see them. They sat at the deal table, with a bottle of gin between them. The flickering light of a rush lamp on the wall cast grotesque shadows on their faces as they leaned together in conspiracy, the very picture of evil incarnate.

"You're to station yourself behind the big old oak tree in the clearing of the spinney. There at the east end. You know where I mean?" Sir Giles asked, and Robinson nodded. "We'll each count out our twelve paces. You keep count with us. And the instant he turns, you fire. Aim for his heart, Bert. You'll only get one shot, and you've got to do it before he shoots, or I'm a dead man. I can't hope to outshoot a sportsman like Raventhorpe. I'll discharge my pistol as well, to make it look as if it was my shot that got him, but I'll aim above his shoulder. In the excitement and confusion, no one will notice. Can I count on you?"

"Ye've chosen your man well." Bert grinned. "I can take the eye out of a pigeon in flight. A man's chest will be like hitting a barn door. Ye can count on me, Sir Giles. But why did you accept a challenge from him, if you don't mind my asking? You might have got out of it, eh?"

"Accept a challenge? I forced the duel on him, the young upstart. He thinks to walk away with her fortune, after I've spent the better part of my life building it up for my son. It's mine as much as hers. She's no right to squander it on him. She's a foolish young thing. She doesn't know what's good for her. It's my job to protect her."

"It's Raventhorpe that's full of mischief, like his father before him," Robinson said ingratiatingly.

She heard the tinkle of golden coins. "Here's a hundred in advance," Sir Giles said. "There'll be another hundred after the deed is done. And if you ever whisper a word of this bargain to a soul, Bert Robinson, I'll hunt you down and shoot you like a dog."

"My word's my bond, Sir Giles," Bert said, and pocketed the money.

A cold sweat beaded Arabella's brow, and her breaths came in shallow gasps. A wave of nausea seized her, but she willed it down. She had to warn Raventhorpe not to come to Chêne Mow. Even now he was on his way here. He might go charging in the front door at any moment, and Bert would murder him before the planned time. What Sir Giles was planning was nothing else but cold-blooded murder. And it was not her he was worried about, it was her money. His rationalizing didn't fool her. She turned to flee, and her elbow bumped a stick of firewood that protruded from a shelf. It knocked a can of nails to the floor in a resounding clatter.

Before she could escape, the kitchen door was flung open and Bert Robinson grabbed her arm. "What's this, then? An eavesdropper!"

She looked into the kitchen, where Sir Giles was staring at her with wary eyes. He

174

didn't bother to rise. "How much have you heard?" he asked.

"Nothing!" she said, much too quickly. She was as white as snow, and trembling from head to foot. "I didn't hear anything, Uncle."

He and Robinson exchanged a grim look. When Sir Giles turned to her again, the wariness had changed to knowledge. "What are you doing here?" he asked.

"Nothing. I'm—nothing."

"You're meeting *him*," Sir Giles said, leaping on the dangerous truth. She looked at the pistol on the table. "As you met him last night. I saw him leaving Chêne Bay. He's had his way with you, hasn't he?"

"No! I promise you he has not!"

"Killing's too good for the likes of him," Robinson declared.

"No! You mustn't!" Arabella exclaimed.

From beyond the door, the rumble of an approaching carriage was heard on the road beyond. "She's meeting him, by gad. That's Raventhorpe, I wager," Robinson said, fingering his pistol.

There was murder in Sir Giles's eyes. "I thought you gave in to that morning wedding a bit too easily," he said. He stood up then and extinguished the rushlight, plunging them into darkness. Arabella could no longer see their faces, to help discern their intentions, but the very air was heavy with menace. She turned to flee, and felt Sir Giles's fingers clamp about her wrist

175

like a manacle. The rumble of the carriage drew nearer. It was at the gateway. She could hear the jingle of the harnesses now as the groom drew to a stop.

"Don't! You mustn't shoot him!" she cried.

Sir Giles had no intention of shooting Raventhorpe in front of Arabella. He quickly scanned his options and said, "If you want your lover to live, tell him you're through with him. Tell him he's not to come back. And you'd best make him believe it, missy. Bert's hard to control when he has a pistol in his hand. There, he's coming in at the front door!" he said, as the sound of footsteps on the veranda echoed within.

"He'd not have seen our light through the hedge," Bert said.

Sir Giles said, "We'll go into the front parlor. Let her have her word with him at the door. And if he doesn't leave like a gentleman when she turns him off, then you know what you must do, Bert. Arabella?" His fingers tightened on her wrist. Even the bone beneath the flesh hurt.

"Yes, I'll turn him off," she said, weak with fear. At that moment she would have agreed to marry Robinson or Sir Giles himself to save bloodshed.

She was led through the dark house, trembling with fear, feeling in her bones that neither she nor Raventhorpe would come out of this alive. Sir Giles never slackened his tight grip on her. If she

176

could only get rid of Alexander temporarily, she would find some way to notify him of the dangerous duel facing him. The important thing now was to convince him she was through with him, because if he once set foot inside the doorway, he would be shot dead. She must act as she had never acted before in her life.

She opened the door a crack and saw him, waiting in the moonlight. Her heart was wrenched to have to let him think for a single moment that she didn't love him to the edge of distraction. "Alexander," she said in a voice as dead as a corpse. He turned and hurried toward her, wearing a smile. "I've changed my mind. I'm sorry, but I'm not going to marry you after all."

"Now, what game is this, my pet?" he laughed easily. "If it's the duel—"

"It's no game!" she said, her voice rising in fear. Having no reason to suspect she was frightened, Raventhorpe mistook her emotion for anger. "You're too hotheaded. I could never marry anyone like you. It was all a game to pay you back for leaving me alone all winter. I'm not marrying you. Just go away and leave me alone."

He stared at her with an expression of disbelief. "Belle, don't say that unless you mean it."

"I do mean it. Go! Go away and never come back. I don't love you. I never did. Just go." Tears streamed down her face, and her voice rose hysterically. It occurred to her that her uncle still planned to murder Raventhorpe. He might lock her up, to prevent her from getting word to him about Robinson. The duel would go forward tomorrow as planned, unless she could stop it. "Go tonight, this very minute," she said. "Go back to London."

Raventhorpe just looked, unable to credit this was the same woman who had loved him last night, who had written to him that very morning asking his help. When he spoke, his tone was high with disbelief. "What have they done to you?"

"I told you not to fight that duel," she said. "If you fight a duel with my uncle—"

"I apologized. It's your uncle you should be reading this lecture. He wouldn't accept my apology."

"You'd better—" She felt the nose of the pistol nudge against her spine. She couldn't warn him about the duel, but perhaps she could convince him to leave. "The duel's off," she said. "My uncle's changed his mind, so you can go back to London without worrying about your precious pride."

"I haven't heard from Almquist of this change of mind."

Again the pistol was pressed firmly against her. "If you fight that duel, I'll never speak to you again. Just go away. Go now, and I'll try not to think so badly of you."

Raventhorpe continued staring in disbelief, there in the moonlight. She was half-hidden by the door. The part of her he could see looked like a demented woman, with wildly staring eyes. He had always known she would dislike the idea of a duel. It had gone against the pluck to agree to meet Sir Giles, but he had no alternative. Damme, he was doing it for her. And this was his thanks. She had made a game of him, to ease her wounded pride over his sojourn in London.

"So Sir Giles has won after all," he said.

"Yes."

Still he stood, thinking, wondering if her uncle was putting some pressure on her, perhaps threatening her with social expulsion or some such foolish thing. "There's a ship leaving Bournemouth tomorrow for Greece. We could make it, Belle. Come with me. Come away with me tonight. You won't have to face your uncle and the neighbors, if that's what bothers you."

"It's you who's bothering me. I was happy until I met you. Go away. Just go away." She slammed the door and fell against it, sobbing.

In the shadows, three pairs of ears waited for the sound of movement beyond the door. There was one rattling bang as Raventhorpe kicked the door, or slammed it with his fist. An echo of some profanity followed the bang, then he strode angrily away. There was the crack of a whip, and the carriage rumbled down the road.

Once Raventhorpe was beyond danger, Arabella's fear congealed to a cold fury. She turned on her uncle. "How dare you make me do this! I'll never marry your precious William, and that I promise you. I know what you're after. My money! I've got your measure now, sir."

"My dear," he said in the same syrupy tone she had been hearing forever, and never before realized it was the voice of hypocrisy. "It was for your own good."

"No, Uncle. It was for your good. I want you out of Chêne Bay by eventide tomorrow, and you may take your son with you. I'll not have you under my roof."

"You forget I am your guardian, Arabella. You are still a minor."

"You forget there are such things as laws in this country," she flashed back, and wrenched the door open. "I don't care if you do manage to steal my fortune. I'd rather live on a bone with Alexander than marry William. I shan't marry him, so don't think it."

A ray of wan moonlight formed a fan in the hallway. It was bright enough to see her uncle nod in Robinson's direction, to see the black muzzle of the gun rise, and point at her. She stared at it a moment, shocked into immobility. He wouldn't dare! But the cold glitter in Sir Giles's eyes told her he would. She made a motion to escape through the open door and Sir Giles's strong arms seized her.

"Best wait until he's gone beyond hearing," he said to Robinson. "'Twould be awkward if he came back."

"It might be for the best," Robinson

said. "A lovers' quarrel... He's a hot-headed rascal, is young Raventhorpe. We chance along and catch him standing over the corpse, we have to shoot him."

"As you wish." Sir Giles nodded. He stepped aside and let Robinson pinion her against the wall.

The clatter of the horses and carriage prevented Raventhorpe from hearing the pistol being fired. Robinson was taking no chance of missing his target in the semi-darkness, and held the gun tightly against Arabella's breast, which muffled the sound.

When she lay on the floor, with her lifeblood soaking into her gown, she heard Robinson say, as if from a great distance, "It seems he's not coming back. Best to leave her here and find her in the morning. With luck, someone may have seen Raventhorpe stopping."

"Put her in the blue room," Sir Giles said. "It will look more like a lovers' quarrel if they're in a bedroom."

Arabella felt a heaviness in her chest as they carried her upstairs. Not a pain, exactly. Her senses were too weak to feel a physical pain. They laid her on the bed, and stood a moment talking, but she did not listen. In the darkness, the voice she heard was Alexander's. *So Sir Giles has won after all.* It couldn't be! She could not be dying without telling Alexander she loved him! She could never rest in peace until he knew, and until the world knew of her uncle's treachery.

But she was dying. This great shining light that came to meet her was death. It was not so frightening as she had thought it would be. It was almost peaceful, welcoming....

In the morning it was Mrs. Meyers who discovered that Arabella was missing and raised the alarm. Before noon, it was learned that Raventhorpe was also gone from his home. There was conjecture that they had run away together. This pleased Sir Giles, and in the dead of night, he and Robinson removed Arabella's body from the blue room at Chêne Mow and buried it in the spinney. If questions were asked later, even if the body was found, who would ever believe it was her loving uncle, who had been willing to risk his life for her, who had killed her? Especially when a more likely suspect was so close at hand.

It was a few days before they heard Raventhorpe had boarded a ship for Greece at Bournemouth, alone. He had returned first to Oldstead Abbey to take his leave of his mother. He gave no real reason for the journey. He just wanted to get away, she said.

At that time, Bert Robinson remembered having seen a tall man with a lady at the weir the night Arabella disappeared. They seemed to be struggling. He thought it a lovers' spat. He had heard a splash, and even heard the lady call for help, but thought the man would rescue her. Sir Giles had the weir dragged, but no trace of the body was found. Arabella's packed parcel of gowns was discovered at Chêne

Mow, and returned in secret to Chêne Bay, where Mrs. Meyers laid them away in trunks in the attic. Sir Giles gave her to understand she had been seriously derelict in her chaperoning of Arabella, and the less said of it, the better. He kindly arranged to find her a position in Scotland, where her lapses were not known.

With no body, and with the influence of Lady Raventhorpe's to impede legal matters, no warrant for Lord Raventhorpe's arrest was ever issued, but the legend grew up in the neighborhood that Arabella had spurned Raventhorpe's advances, and in a fit of passion, he had drowned her in the weir to prevent her from marrying Throckley. A distraught serving girl, sneaking home through the meadow from a meeting with her lover, was frightened by a rabbit in the meadow, and reported seeing Arabella's ghost. Ere long, other people sighted her ghost as well, and even heard it wailing.

Sir Giles and William Throckley draped their hats and sleeves with crape, and went into deep mourning. The door of Chêne Bay bore its funereal hatchment, and a mourning service was held at the church, none of which hastened the transfer of Arabella's fortune into their eager hands. That did not happen until the requisite seven years were up, at which time Arabella was proclaimed legally dead, and Sir Giles became the owner of the estate he had so long coveted.

Chapter Eighteen

When I looked up from the litter of hastily scribbled sheets on the table, I could scarcely believe it was midnight. My shoulders and neck ached, and my vision was blurred from fatigue. How many days had I spent in this little cottage, transcribing the story that seemed to come to me from nowhere—from the air, or Arabella's spirit, or from the cottage itself?

This table I sat at was the same table at which Sir Giles and Bert Robinson had planned Raventhorpe's murder. It was through that kitchen window that Arabella had peered, and seen them plotting the evil deed. That dark smudge by the edge of the cupboard was where the rushlight had hung, casting its shadows on the conspirators. And the blue bedroom where I slept was the room where Arabella had been taken to die. No wonder it had felt unwelcoming!

My thoughts were sad, but the story was coming along splendidly. I could hardly wait for morning to discover what came next. Arabella's tale was finished, and if the novel was to continue, the plot must follow Raventhorpe to Greece and Italy, and delve into his amorous career there. I felt an angry sting to even contemplate him with other women, his lips burning theirs, his tongue whispering silken lies.

I climbed the stairs and fell wearily into bed. My sleep that night was dreamless. Usually the general idea for the next day's writing came to me while I slept. At least I did not dream of the dark maze. When I sat down to work the next morning, I found myself staring at the blank page, not knowing what to write. I had no mental image of Raventhorpe dashing off to Bournemouth. Was he angry, sad? What did the ship look like? Did he take his carriage and groom on board with him? If not, what did he do with them? I riffled my hands through my hair, and at last decided I needed a break from writing. The sun was shining. I'd drive to Lyndhurst and buy my groceries.

When I passed Mollie's office, I dropped in to say hello. She was bent over her desk, working. "Belle!" she exclaimed. "Long time no see. What have you been doing with yourself?"

"I've been busy writing."

Her green eyes examined me closely. "You look tuckered out, my girl. You've been working too hard. You should get about and see the countryside while you're here. I'll tell you what, why don't you visit Chêne Bay this afternoon? You can check and see you've got the details of the house right. It's the day for tours. I'd go with you, but I'm snowed under in paperwork."

"I might do that."

As Mollie was so busy, I soon left to do my shopping. At home, I put away my

185

groceries and went out to the garden and began pulling weeds, which Beezle joyfully scattered far and wide. It was soothing, getting my hands in the earth. When my back began to complain of bending over, I went inside for lunch. I was surprised to see it was only eleven o'clock. How long the day seemed when I wasn't writing.

I decided to take the tour of Chêne Bay after all. To pass the time until lunch, I tidied up the cottage. This took half an hour. I showered and changed for the house tour. By the time I had made a sandwich and eaten it, a tourist bus had driven up to Chêne Bay, so I walked up the hill to join the tour.

The sense of familiarity that engulfed me was easy to explain. I had been looking at those columns for a week now. The tour guide, wearing a black evening suit, was waiting at the door. He was about twenty years old. His accent suggested that he was from one of the better universities. He welcomed me with a handshake, told me his name was Warwick, and said if I'd just step into the gold saloon, the tour would begin presently.

There were about two dozen people waiting, half a dozen of them Americans, with a smattering of German and some young English rock fans who had come to see where Ivan the Terrible lived. Warwick soon entered and began to expound on the architecture, furnishings, and artworks. Every second word was "sadly." Sadly the original Gainsborough paintings had been sold to pay death duties some years before; sadly the Italian mural had been painted over, and unfortunately the current owner had accidentally broken a Canaletto bust of Princess Charlotte which formerly occupied a pedestal that at present held the egglike head of a woman by Brancusi. Its stark modernity jarred with the surroundings.

We were taken through a long dining hall, the same one where Arabella had had her last uncomfortable meal, with William taking too much wine. We toured the library and a picture gallery, which held paintings on which the oil was scarcely dry. They were all modern nudes of unlikely contours, in various preposterous positions and colors.

One of the rock fans asked, "Can we see him—Ivan?"

Sadly, Ivan was in London, "but if you wish to purchase posters or T-shirts, they will be available upon leaving."

How very odd life is, that the house where Arabella lived, and the property for which Sir Giles had schemed and murdered, should end up as a shop selling cheap T-shirts and posters of a rock star. *Sic transit gloria mundi.*

I decided to leave. Nothing was as I had expected. The furnishings clashed, destroying the beauty of the architecture. I felt no tinglings of familiarity, but only a sense of claustrophobia.

Warwick said, "And now for the sleeping quarters. We will be touring only the east wing. The present owner has left it intact, making his own quarters in the west wing. You will see Arabella Comstock's bedchamber. She is the ghost who walks the meadow, wailing for her lover, the infamous Vanejul of local legend. The room still holds her bed and clothespress."

I came to attention then and followed him up the gracefully curving staircase as he gave more statistics. There were carvings in the upper hallway, by Grinling Gibbons. At the top of the staircase, I looked down a long hallway, pierced at intervals with mullioned windows. My eye stopped at the third door on the left. That was Arabella's room. I don't know how I knew, but I knew. First we toured a few other chambers, with period furniture and canopied beds and hand-painted Chinese wallpaper, but I hardly glanced at them. I was trying to conjure up an image of Arabella's room. If I knew what it was like before seeing it, then I knew more than I should, because I had seen no photograph of it. When I had written of Arabella in her room, she seemed to exist in a sort of fog.

I closed my eyes and concentrated until an image formed inside my head. First came a hazy impression of yellow and green, soon firming to a room hung with pale green paper, on which clusters of cherries and hummingbirds hung suspended. On the wall opposite the doorway there was a pair of windows, looking out on the park. Beneath them a graceful chaise longue covered in tufted green velvet spread invitingly. A canopied bed sat against the left wall. On the right, there stood a matching desk and toilet table in apple green with white knobs.

Warwick led us to the third doorway and flung it open. I entered and found myself gazing at a pair of windows with a faded green chaise longue below them. The room was as I had seen it in my mind's eye, but grown fatigued with the passing of time, and with a noticeable hole where, sadly, the Italian toilet table and desk had been removed. The honking voice of Warwick enumerating periods of furnishings and dates passed over me as I stood, transfixed. I could almost see the reflection of Arabella's little heart-shaped face smiling at me from the mirror. It was an awesomely strange experience to have confirmed what I already knew instinctively in my deepest heart of hearts.

Warwick led us to a portrait on the far wall. "And here is a likeness of Arabella Comstock taken in her sixteenth year by a local artist, James Thorndyke. It was intended as a wedding gift to her husband-to-be." I gazed at it, wondering if the artist was some ancestor of Henry Thorndyke. It was the original from which the picture in the history of the Raventhorpes had been taken. Probably the only likeness of her ever taken from life.

189

As it was larger than the reproduction, it was possible to make out more details.

The painting was done in the romantic style of Watteau, against a backdrop of idealized trees. Arabella looked so very young. She wore her golden curls scooped up on the back of her head, with tendrils playing about her cheeks and the pearl teardrops hanging at her ears. A white shawl was about her shoulders, with a blue gown beneath. But it was at her eyes that I gazed. They were blue, long-lashed, and wearing the saddest expression, almost as if she had foreseen her fate. It was odd, for in the reproduction in the book, her eyes had looked mischievous.

While I stood there, suspended in time, I felt in my heart what it was Arabella wanted of me: to prove who had really murdered her, to remove for all time the cloud of suspicion that hung over Raventhorpe. But how on earth was I to prove a crime that had been committed nearly two hundred years ago?

Where did one even begin such an impossible task? The witnesses, if any, were long dead. The clues had turned to dust. The body had never been recovered. And on top of it all, a cover-up story had been circulating for nearly two centuries to further muddy the waters. It would take a miracle to unravel all the suppositions and lies that existed.

But still, I knew I must do it. Miracles can happen.

Chapter Nineteen

I went back to Chêne Mow, arranged the scattered sheets of the unfinished novel into a pile, and sat at the deal table. To accomplish this daunting task, I must set about it in an orderly fashion. What proof, if any, existed for the facts I knew that the rest of the world did not? I knew that Bert Robinson had lied about seeing Vanejul push Arabella into the weir. Her remains were not there; they were buried, presumably in some quiet corner of the estate. Not near any crop or pasture or garden, not in open land. In a woods, then... Sir Giles had spoken of the duel taking place in the spinney.

Did the spinney still exist, or had some house been built over it during the passing of time? If I could find her mortal remains, I could prove that she had been shot. That would at least disprove the commonly held theory, and perhaps lead to more investigation.

The lovers had exchanged notes that last day. Arabella's letter to Raventhorpe might be at Oldstead or in Greece or tossed in the ocean in a fit of pique. What had Arabella done with the note Raventhorpe sent her? A young lady in love might have kept her billets-doux. Maybe hidden in her desk, or slid between the pages of a book.

I poured a glass of sherry and sat, trying to make sense of this whole situation.
If Arabella had been writing her story
through me, then that would explain why
I had run dry. She had no idea what happened to Raventhorpe after she was shot,
so she could not lead me on his trip
abroad. But she could help me find evidence
of her murder. The insight that she was
buried in the spinney must have come
from her. If the spinney still existed, it
should be possible to find it. I had seen a
copse from Arabella's bedroom window.
In the clearing by the big oak, Sir Giles
had mentioned as a private spot for the duel,
and it could provide a private burial
ground as well. The English oak was known
for its longevity. Some of the largest oak
trees in England were believed to have
been here since Saxon times. If it was
known as "the big oak" nearly two hundred
years ago, it would certainly stand out
now. The clearing, however, might hold fully
grown trees by this time.

Becoming restless, I decided I would go
to the spinney and look for the big oak while
it was still daylight. I took Beezle for company. Arabella's room was in the east
wing, so I skirted the east side of the
park. A pair of swallows wheeled in the blue
sky above. In fancy, I imagined they were
Arabella and Raventhorpe, watching over
me. A walk of twenty minutes brought
me to the spinney. It was densely grown.
The pathway through it would begin

on the side nearest the house, for the convenience of the family. Peering up at the ancient pile of stones, I darted forward along the tree line and found the path just where common sense told me it would be, convenient to the house. It was still open, and hoof marks in dried mud told me it was still in use as a horse trail.

I entered warily. High above, leaves rustled in the breeze. In small clearings, wildflowers grew and an occasional forest creature rustled the fallen leaves. It was as peaceful as a graveyard. I examined the trees at every clearing. Several of them were oak, but not big enough to be the one I sought.

It should tower high above the others. I looked all around, unable to see the tree for the forest. Just as I was about to continue along the path, I noticed one treetop to the right that did soar noticeably above the others. I followed the path and soon reached a small clearing. At its edge, a giant old oak towered like a cathedral. Its trunk was thick, its branches gnarled and intertwined. Here—this was the spot Robinson had buried her. I could almost feel the earth tremble beneath me. But it was a largish clearing, roughly thirty feet square. To excavate the whole place would take weeks.

Could I pinpoint the grave more closely? He would not have dug too close to the oak, where the roots would make it difficult. Yet not in the middle of the clearing either, where a fresh grave would stand out. These spinneys were used for sheltering game birds, so the poachers would often be here. Around the edge then. I sat on a gray flat-topped rock as big as a throne, mentally selecting the most inconspicuous spot for a grave. Beezle was no help. He curled up at my feet.

I thought of poor Arabella, lying all these years without even a headstone to honor her last resting place. It was a few moments before it occurred to me that I might be sitting on her headstone. Rolling a large rock over the freshly dug grave would be a good way of concealing it—and it would make digging her up difficult, if any poacher became curious about the newly turned earth. I leapt up and examined the rock. The passage of time had imbued it with an ageless, immovable quality. Grass and weeds and a few wildflowers covered the earth, making it appear like the rest of the clearing.

I could only test my theory by digging, and for that, I required Ivan's permission. As Mollie knew him, I must ask her to help me. I rose and darted back along the path, out into the park and down the hill to Chêne Mow, with Beezle bounding at my heels. I phoned Mollie just as she was leaving the office.

"Mollie, it's Belle. Can I see you? It's important. Come here for supper. Are you busy?"

She sensed my eagerness. "I'll be there in twenty minutes," she said.

I flung together a hasty meal. Pasta was the easiest thing. I made chicken fettuccine and a salad. I hastily chilled a bottle of white wine in the freezer, and when Mollie arrived, I served it while the sauce simmered.

"Oh, thank you, dear. This looks super. Did you take the tour of Chêne Bay?" she asked, kicking off her high heels and rubbing her swollen toes with the heel of the other foot.

"Yes, it was so strange. I knew exactly what Arabella's room would be like before I saw it. Mollie, I need your help. I know where Arabella's body is. She's not in the lake. Bert Robinson made up that story. She's buried in the spinney."

Mollie's green eyes sparkled with interest. "How do you know? And who's Bert Robinson?"

I unburdened myself to her, thankful that she was a believer, because the story sounded so far-fetched, I was half-ashamed to relate it. But Mollie took it all in her stride.

"I don't think Ivan would object," she said. "He's very much attuned to occult matters. But he wouldn't want a lot of gawkers interrupting his privacy."

"The more private, the better, but we'll need one man to help us move the big rock. Do you think Henry Thorndyke might give us a hand?"

"I'll ask him, but first I'll have to give Ivan a buzz. I have his unlisted London number."

She called and got an answering service. He was out for the evening. She asked him to call her back. "He'll call," she said complacently. "He fancies me. No point calling Henry until we hear back from Ivan. Is there anything else we could be getting on with in the meanwhile?"

I mentioned the note Arabella had written Raventhorpe asking him to apologize to her uncle, and more important, his reply. She received that note on the very day of her murder.

Remembering my novel's interpretation of that day, I said, "It might be in her desk. Emily has her desk."

"You're thinking there might be a secret compartment?"

The open drawer was there, inside my head. I could almost feel myself reach to the rear of that scented, pinkish drawer. "At the back of the small drawer on the right," I said.

"Ah!" Mollie smiled to see me practicing my skills.

"Emily told me to let her know if she could help me."

Mollie said, "We'll drop in on her after dinner."

I knew Mollie must be hungry after her busy day, and put the pasta on to boil. My dinner was a success. Strangely, we didn't talk much about Arabella and

Raventhorpe. Mollie offered to help with the dishes, but I made her sit on the sofa while I put them to soak. When I returned, she had called Emily. We were to see her at eight-thirty.

Chapter Twenty

Emily was waiting for us. Sensing some drama, she had dressed in a floor-length gown of mulberry hue, garnished with long ropes of pearls that were surely fake, though they looked real. She looked regal, like a dowager from a Regency novel.

"Come in, come in," she chirped merrily.

We followed her to the same comfortably shabby parlor where she had served me tea, and we took up our places. "I have been wondering," she said, peering at me with brightly curious eyes, "has the locket worked for you?"

"Like a charm." I lifted it to show her I wore it constantly. "I've been wondering why you lent it to me, Emily."

"Oh, come, my dear," she chided gently. "We both know Arabella wanted you to have it, and you wanted it, too. There must have been a reason."

"Emily is clairvoyant," Mollie said. "She just knows these things. We all come to Emily when we run a cropper in our psychic lives. She's a miracle, no question."

I cleared my throat and said, "As a matter of fact, it has worked miracles for me."

"I knew it!" Emily crowed. "The name could not be a mere coincidence. Your full name is Arabella, isn't it?"

"No! My name is Belle Marie Savage."

"But you must be some kin to her. Belle is not a common name for your generation. Why, I cannot think of a single woman my own age with the name. It has been out of style forever."

I realized I didn't know anyone else with my name. "I was called after my aunt," I explained. "How could I be related to Arabella? I'm not even English. I'm from the States."

"I know where you are from, dear. I've been dredging through the family records. One branch of Arabella's family went to America after the war, in 1820. They settled in the colonies."

"I have no relatives called Comstock, as far as I know. My mother's maiden name was Dalby. Eve Dalby."

"There you are then!" Emily smiled. "Arabella's grandmother was a Dalby before marriage. And her first cousin, Albert, emigrated to America. I'm sure I saw an Eve in the records, too. You are obviously related to Arabella, and to me. Isn't that nice?"

A sense of wonder seized me. A woman I had never heard of, a whole ocean and centuries away, had found me, and reached out to me. In spite of the years separating us, the connection moved me profoundly. We were kin; some trace of Arabella's blood flowed in my veins, mingling with that of past generations, a living link between us. How natural that she should sense the kinship when fate placed me at Chêne Mow—sister calling to sister. It had been in the stars from the beginning of time that I should come here to rescue her.

"That is why Raventhorpe chose you, when we called up his spirit at the séance," Emily explained. "He sensed that trace of Arabella in you."

"You know what is strange," I said, "is that I have seen Raventhorpe, yet I feel my story is coming from Arabella, and I have not actually seen her."

"The locket," Emily said with a shrug. "But that is not why you are here. Mollie said something about the desk."

"Belle thinks there's a secret compartment," Mollie explained, and explained also why we wanted to find the note, if there was one there. I told Emily the whole story, about Arabella being murdered by her uncle and Robinson.

Emily said, "I never believed for a moment that Raventhorpe killed her. I could see him killing William in a fit of jet black jealousy, or Sir Giles for that matter, but certainly not Arabella. Shall we go to the desk?"

We went, huddling together like conspirators, to the apple green desk with the flowers painted on the front, and the porcelain knobs. I walked forward and reached out for the small right-hand drawer. My fingers were trembling. There wasn't a sound in the room. Even breaths were suspended as I reached out and drew the drawer toward me. It did not come out as far as the middle drawer had. This seemed auspicious. There was some sort of catch holding it partly closed.

"Tap the false back of the drawer," Emily suggested. She and Mollie had advanced to look over my shoulder.

"No," I said, and reached for the knob. I turned it to the right. I had to push quite hard, for the mechanism had become rusted from age. With a little squawk, the knob turned, and the false back fell forward, revealing a pile of letters tied together with a faded blue satin ribbon. Emily emitted a strangled gasp and reached for the letters. Legally they were hers.

Was it mere haste or forgetfulness that had caused Arabella to leave her billets-doux behind when she fled from Chêne Bay? Or had destiny guided her hand, leaving this clue to be unearthed later? Emily took the letters back to the morning parlor and shuffled quickly through them. She opened the first and read it silently to herself. "Yes, they are from him," she said, smiling at what she had read. "Love letters. Very touching. You must take good care of them, Belle."

Then she handed them to me with a ceremonious nod, and I accepted them in the same manner, as though we were ambassadors exchanging honors. Mollie made vociferous objections, as well she might. Emily let her read the first one, then took it back and gave it to me, with a conspiratorial smile.

"You will decide how much of them is for public perusal," she said.

"You mean I can take them home?"

"Take them and give them a good read, then bring them back. They are quite valuable, I should think. Now, was there anything else?"

Mollie mentioned digging up the grave in the spinney. "Henry will be glad to help," Emily said. "He takes a keen interest in Arabella. His ancestor painted many of the family portraits at Chêne Bay, including Arabella's. As to the disinterment, the police must be notified first."

"We needn't call it a disinterment," Mollie said. "As far as the authorities know, we are just digging a hole in a spinney to plant a tree. You don't need permission for that."

"You *are* clever, Mollie," Emily said.

Meanwhile I was on nettles to get home and read the letters. We declined an offer of tea, and as soon as politely possible, I suggested that Mollie and I should be going. Emily, kind soul that she was, did not detain us.

When we reached Chêne Mow, Mollie had work to do at home and left without coming in. I took my precious letters inside, locked the door, and went to the deal table to study them.

It didn't feel right. It seemed there should be some sense of ceremony. I decided to read them by candlelight, as Arabella would have read them, all those years ago. There were candles in a drawer in the kitchen, and I arranged them in holders on the table. It still felt wrong. I glanced down at my jeans, and suddenly knew what was the matter.

I went upstairs and changed into my blue dress. With a thought of the portrait of Arabella at Chêne Bay, I added a white shawl around my shoulders. In the shadowed mirror, I looked a little like her. It was easy to believe we really were distant cousins. I arranged my hair as Arabella wore hers in the painting, letting a few strands tumble forward. There—that was more or less how Arabella looked when she read her love letters.

I smiled at my own folly. I was pretending I was her, Arabella. When I read those tender love letters, I wanted to pretend they were written to me, that Raventhorpe was pouring his heart out to me. That he loved me, as I had come to love him. Was there ever such a fool, falling in love with a man who had been dead for nearly two centuries? I went below, drew a chair up to the table, and opened the first letter.

Chapter Twenty-one

The paper had become sere and yellowed with age. I carefully opened the first letter and gazed at the handwriting. It was the same script I had seen in my mind's eye when I wrote of Raventhorpe's last note to Arabella: a fluidly elegant script, with flourishes.

I read:

May, two of the morning, and I have just left you, Arabella Comstock, after a most indiscreet rendezvous. I do love indiscretion, don't you? It adds a certain *je ne sais quoi* to the most mundane of meetings. Throw in a scenic waterfall, a beautiful young lady, a forbidding guardian, and I shall soon find myself in love—whatever *that* may mean. I have always considered love a sort of amiable madness, a temporary euphoria, like winning a lottery.

I wondered how Arabella had reacted to that "temporary."

He rambled on for the better part of a page in the same light vein, more or less mocking himself and love. In the next letter, he was replying to Arabella's objections. As I expected, she had quizzed him about that "temporary." He replied blunt-

203

ly, "I do not ascribe any unusual meaning to the word. I mean impermanent, transient, passing. Not forever." There was a warning for her, and a challenge!

It seemed she had also objected to "most mundane of meetings."

I did not call *our* meeting mundane, shrew! Naturally any meeting between such incomparables as you and I must be ultra-mundane. *Äa va sans dire.* I do hope you speak French? How can one hope to carry on a romantic correspondence in English? Total comprehension reveals the paucity of our imagination and the tawdriness of our desires. We require the obfuscation of a foreign tongue to shroud our meaning in glamour. According to Henry V of France, one confers with men in French, with horses in German, and with ladies in Italian, so I ought to be writing in Italian—but I fear that would provide too much in the way of obfuscation. According to all the rules of polite society, I really ought not to be writing at all to such a young miss. Going to be fifteen next month! Good God! You are an infant! Why can you not look your age, and save me from temptation? That guardian ought to order you to put your hair down and your skirts up, like a good little girl.

In the next one he addressed her as

"My dearest Arabella," and wrote:

No French at all? *Quella honte!* (For shame!) I daresay you have been wasting your time sewing and reading the Bible, when you ought to have been learning more useful arts—like flirting, and waltzing, and speaking French. Flirting and waltzing are innate to young ladies; they will come soon enough without effort. As to French, I have made a list of phrases required in polite society. You may ignore them, with the exception of *on dit*, for if our meetings should be discovered, we would be in some danger of becoming one of those pestilential things, "they say." Who are these *ons* who will forever be finding wickedness in all one's harmless pleasures? Is the whole world populated with Mrs. Grundys?

The words you will require are as follows: love—*amour*; my darling—*mon cher*; always or forever—*toujours*; I love you—*je t'adore* (to be used only with the greatest discretion, i.e., to Lord Raventhorpe); *argent*—money; and most important of all, yes—*oui*. The above words can be combined in sentence form, e.g. *"Ah oui, mon cher amour, je t'adore."* This evening we shall practise the appropriate gestures to accompany the words, and perhaps teach you a new one. Or perhaps not. Nearly fifteen! Egads.

As I read on through the letters, the bantering tone gradually became more serious.

You want to hear it in English? Very well then, I love you. Or if this be not love, then I am extremely ill of an undiagnosed disease, for I can neither eat nor sleep nor pay the least heed to business. I actually paid my tailor yesterday, and I have not had his bill above three months. If I cannot have you soon, I shall take to poetry, and make a demmed fool of myself. Once a man has fallen into poesy, the only cure is an early death. There is something just a little ludicrous in an aged poet, all passion spent, rhyming on, don't you think? Truly, though, Belle, you are fifteen now, and therefore in your sixteenth year. Is that too young? Cleopatra was a queen at that age. At least I think it was Cleopatra, though it may have been a queen of France.

He wrote in a lighthearted vein about the everyday occurrences of his life, telling her of a tumble he had taken from a horse.

Not satisfied with throwing me to the ground, the bleater lifted his head and uttered a whinnying laugh at my expense, while the village looked on, convulsed in laughter. I was forced into a gri-

206

macing smile, too, for I would not satisfy my audience to fly into a pelter in public like a comic actor in a second-rate play, which was what they expected of a Raventhorpe. But I have had the last laugh. I sold the brute to Mr. Hopkins (weight 285 pounds). That will teach the boiler to make sport of me. May his spine bend under the weight of his new burden, then he will miss me, and the bushels of apples I fed the ingrate.

There, now I have revealed one of my less attractive sides to you. Do you still think me kind and generous? The little locket was not generosity, it was my way of staking a claim to you, as I cannot yet put a ring on your finger.

There was a postscript. "You are not to go drawing any parallels between my treatment of recalcitrant horses and recalcitrant ladies. I have never sold Hopkins a lady in my life. I am in too much awe of his wife. She weights 290 pounds."

With a smile I put the letter aside and lifted another. The date showed me some time had passed since his last letter. I wished I could know what had happened at their meetings in the interval. It seemed the offer of marriage had been made and accepted.

He wrote:

My darling Belle:

How time drags when I am away from

you. If every day is to last a month, we shall be old and gray before you are mine. How fine it would be if the next eight months would flee quickly, and Time save its lagging gait for after we are married. Then I would have no objection if Time should stand still. But it never does when I am with you. I fear that I shall awake one morning, expecting to see my young bride by my side, and find an elderly dame with gray hair, and myself too feeble to love her as I would like. Our lives will have flitted by while we blinked.

Was it really three of the morning when you got to bed last night? That means we spent three hours together. Where did the time go? It is all one glorious golden mist in my memory. Did I imagine you saying you loved me to distraction? Did I have the wits to tell you I feel the same? I do, my darling.

From the first moment I looked across the room and saw your pretty, prissy little face, with your flashing eyes trying not to look at me, I felt my fate was sealed. And what a pretty fate it is. My only regret is that we must meet in secret. Or do I regret it? It will be something to tell our children. Make that our grown children. We would not want to lead innocent youngsters astray, for they will always go a pace beyond the bounds set by their parents. I wonder the world has no account of Bluebeard's children, and Casanova's, and Don Juan's.

I felt a stab of regret to know they had not even enjoyed that one blink of married bliss. Raventhorpe never had awakened with his young bride by his side, and they had left no children for posterity.

The stack of letters was growing thin. Raventhorpe mentioned disliking to drag Arabella out in inclement weather to meet by the weir. It was fast approaching the time when they had argued about it, and Raventhorpe had dashed off to London. I knew it was frustration and concern for her safety as much as dislike of the cold that made him impatient. Things might have turned out quite differently if they had gone on meeting, and he had seduced her. The temptation must have been strong, and I admired Raventhorpe's control in acting the gentleman.

He did not write after their row, when he went to London to wait out the winter. There was only one more letter. If it did not deal with their meeting at Chêne Mow to elope, then I had nothing in writing to substantiate what had happened.

I opened the last letter and read the familiar words:

My own dear Belle:
    This is intolerable! Your uncle would not accept an apology. It is clear he wants to kill me by fair means or foul. As to forc-

ing you to marry William! I shall meet you at midnight tonight at Chêne Mow, as you suggest, and take you—and all your new finery—to Oldstead to stay for the nonce. But pray do not ask me to cry craven on the duel. I, and in some collateral way you, would carry the shame of cowardice with us until death. Neither pride nor common sense recommends that course to me. I shall not let Throckley make a William of me.

I shall meet your uncle, but I shall not kill him. A wound, high on the shoulder, will teach him a lesson without putting him in his grave. Almquist is awake on all suits. He will see there is no trickery in the affair. I would give a year of my life to avoid this duel. That is one disgrace I have managed to avoid until now. Outside of war or some chance heroic deed, there is no honor in killing or being killed. We shall meet at Chêne Mow at midnight, and soon we shall be together for good. Don't, I beg of you, do anything foolish, like confronting Sir Giles on your own. All our future happiness depends on your discretion. All my love, always.

Toujours,
Alexander.

The words were exactly as I had written.

I read the letter twice and set it aside. It certainly gave a clear idea of Sir Giles's intentions. Raventhorpe had said in so many words that Sir Giles was forcing Arabella to marry William. That would explode the theory that she loved William, and Raventhorpe had been blind with jealousy. It also said that Sir Giles meant to kill him. But it was not Raventhorpe who had been killed. It was Arabella. Still, this letter and Arabella's corpse with a bullet in it would certainly go a long way toward exonerating Raventhorpe.

One reading was not enough. I turned to the first billet-doux and read them all through again, envying Arabella her dashing lover. When he addressed her as his dearest Belle, I felt he was writing to me, and my heart swelled with joy. No wonder she roamed the meadow, grieving her loss. Who would not howl in rage at such an injustice?

Wrapped up in the letters, I did not notice at first that the room had grown warm. When I glanced up, I saw he had come back. A charge of adrenaline surged through me, setting my heart racing.

He looked at me with sad, dark eyes.

"You look lovely tonight, Belle," he said softly. I touched my hands to my hair in a self-conscious, preening gesture. "Did you wear a skirt because I asked you to?"

"It seemed appropriate," I said evasively.

His smile stretched to a grin. "After all we have been to one another, you still

211

won't admit you dressed like this to please me."

I blushed in pleasure, to hear I meant so much to him. "I have been reading your letters."

"So I see. I daresay they sound like the gushings of a schoolboy. I was very young when I wrote that treacle, and very much in love."

"They sound fine, even after all these years. Why have you stayed away so long?"

"Was it so long?" he asked, surprised. "There is no accounting for time here. You blink, and miss a generation or two. I remember ladies wearing decent long gowns, then I awoke one morning and they had all chopped off their hair and were exposing their knees and dancing like beheaded chickens. There was a war in the interim, I think," he said vaguely. "Yes, there must have been a war, for I remember being in a trench with mud to my knees. It was almost a relief when the bullet came, though I was only nineteen, with another life ahead of me. We won the war? Did we?"

The chopped hair and the dance, the Charleston apparently, told me he meant World War I. "Yes, and the next."

"Another war?" He shook his head. "Will we never learn?"

"Are you saying you were reincarnated? Your spirit has inhabited various bodies?"

"I suppose that is what happens. The blank spaces, perhaps, are when we are free of mortal cages. I am really not very clear on the details. We are told nothing. It is *chacun pour soi* here."

"Have you never encountered Arabella in all the years since your death?"

"No, I have not seen her."

"You might have made the effort to look," I chided.

"Good God," he said angrily, "do you think I haven't looked the world over for her? You've no idea the herd of human remnants wandering about here. She is avoiding me; that much is clear."

"No, she is not," I said calmly but firmly. "I am sure she is looking for you. Perhaps you are incarnated at different times."

"Why do you say she is looking for me?" he asked. A glint of hope lit his dark eyes.

"She is looking for you. Trust me."

"Trust *you*?" he said, anger flaring suddenly. "I'd as soon trust a fox with a chicken."

"I am trying to help you," I said curtly. I wanted to ask why he was angry, but there were more important things to discover, and he might vanish at any time. I said, "Do you know where they buried Arabella?"

"Surely her grave is in the local church yard, is it not?" He assumed an expression of ennui, but it did not conceal the bitterness

213

of his tone. "Try the Throckley mausoleum. That is where Mrs. William Throckley's mortal remains would be resting."

"She didn't marry William. Actually, they never found her body!"

He stared, as if I were mad. "What do you mean?"

"She never married William. Raventhorpe, did you not know?"

"I—she didn't marry him? Are you sure? I know she sent me off, after begging me to rescue her. But are you saying—what *are* you saying, Belle?" He gazed at me with such fierce intensity that I was almost frightened. His whole body glimmered more brightly. "What did they do to her?"

"Sir Giles murdered her that same night she sent you away from Chêne Mow. She only sent you off to save your life. They meant to shoot you, too." I gave him a brief account of what I had written, and believed to be true. As I related the tragic tale, he listened as one in a trance. A film of moisture pooled in his eyes, but tears did not fall. He sat like a statue until I had finished, then he spoke.

"Oh God!" It was a howl of outrage. "All these years I have cursed and hated that woman, and myself for loving her in spite of all. And now you tell me this, that she gave her life for me. If I had only known, we might have contrived to be together ere now. I *should* have known. I *did* suspect some chicanery, but she told me to my face she loved William. I thought she had been making a game of me, paying me back for going to London that winter. I only went to keep from harming her. She was such an innocent; she had no notion how she inflamed me. But you mean Throckley got away with it? He was never brought to justice?"

"Everyone thinks *you* killed her, Raventhorpe."

He stared as if he couldn't understand. "I? Why would I kill the woman I loved dearer than life itself? I left England, which I loved second only to Belle, to avoid hurting her. I could not trust my temper. We Raventhorpes are cursed with a hot temper, you must know. It was a strong temptation to put a bullet through William's spleen. I wanted an ocean between us, to prevent killing him, for her sake."

"Did no one write to tell you of her death?"

"My only contacts in England were my publisher, my man of business, and Mama. Neither Murray nor Jenkins knew anything about Belle, and Mama's letters were infrequent. I did think it odd she urged me to remain abroad. She didn't tell me what had happened to Belle. I cannot believe she thought I killed her. Mama knew I loved her. She knew I meant to bring her to Oldstead and marry her. I went back to Oldstead that night, to make preparations to leave the country. I told her Belle had jilted me, and the reason. When Belle's death was reported, she feared I would come

215

back and kill William or Sir Giles, or both. That is why she kept it a secret from me. She knew her son well."

"And you don't know where Belle is buried?"

He just shook his head. "I wouldn't give her the satisfaction of looking for her grave, much as I wanted to see it. I only know I wasted that life, frittered it away in idleness and dissipation, trying to forget. I cursed her inconstancy, and used it as an excuse to avoid any serious writing. What did it matter? There was no honor, no justice, no common sense in the world, so I wrote driveling nonsense of what I had seen and done, and became a byword for lechery. Vanejul, when I might have been remembered as Raventhorpe, the poet."

"You are remembered," I said sadly, though in truth he was remembered as Vanejul.

"I am best forgotten. But it is mere childishness to blame my behavior on Belle. Every man is responsible for his own life. That, at least, is made painfully clear to us here. Rationalizations have no currency in the afterlife." He glanced and saw Professor Thumm's book on the end of the table. "That is about me?" he asked, interested in spite of himself.

"Yes, would you like to see it?"

"No, thank you. I have a notion what it will say. A minor poet in the satirical vein, a clever turn of phrase that appeals to the immature of all ages, but lacking the depth of true genius. What really bothers me, you know, is that I would like to have immortalized my Belle as she deserved, as Dante immortalized Beatrice, and Petrarch did Laura. But at best we were Romeo and Juliet. I never did think that one of Shakespeare's better plays, though anything by him is better than almost anything by any other playwright. I hoped I might meet him, but no doubt he has found eternal rest. This wandering from body to body is a punishment for us unworthy souls, you know."

He looked at me with his dark, sorrowful eyes, and tried to smile. "Live the good life, Belle. Do what fate intended you to do, or you will pay a horrific price. The eternal wanderer, in search of redemption."

"I don't know what I am meant to do."

"You will know, one day. I feel a strange peace coming on me, now that you have told me about Belle. Perhaps it was my hatred that kept me from finding eternal peace. Now that I understand, and have forgiven her, I feel the anger ebb. Would it not be strange if it was my own intransigence that has kept me wandering through time, and not my wicked past? We really know so little about the workings of the infinite power."

"Perhaps it was my job to help you," I said. "The thing I was to do on earth."

"There will be business of your own to tend to as well, though perhaps my salvation was a part of it." I watched in frustration as he began to fade. "If you have brought us together, that is no mean accomplishment." His voice was fading, too, becoming a whisper. I was not even sure if I heard him right, but I liked to think that was what he said, that I had brought them together.

I felt a light breeze on my lips, a phantom kiss and a whispered "Thank you, my dear Belle."

Then he was gone, and I sat on alone for a long time, rereading the letters and wishing they had been written to me. It was much later when I went up to bed.

Chapter Twenty-two

I fell at once into a profound sleep. It was much later in the night when I was awakened by the touch of love. Whether it was real or a dream of unparalleled clarity, I did not know then, nor can I say with absolute certainty to this day, but I do not think it was a dream. In any case, I was with Raventhorpe once more. He was there, folding me in his warmth, nuzzling my throat with his warm lips, moving his fingers luxuriantly through my hair, and calling me his own darling Belle. It was what I had wanted from the first time I met him—longer. I had wanted him before ever I saw his face, or knew his lineaments. He was the ideal born in the bone and sought throughout life.

I sensed in him an answer to the bottomless mystery of all my life. He was my other half, the unlived portion of my heart and soul, which held a promise of fulfillment. All the reckless daring I lacked would come from him, bringing unimagined splendor to my dull existence. He had been so near from the beginning, an innate desire that hovered always at the edge of consciousness, the "do I dare?" of my life. The shadow of my days, and the illumination of my nights, the answer sought but never found, the yearning desire never fulfilled.

I wanted to be Arabella, and he wanted so much to reclaim her that he believed I was. One atomy of her was enough to inflame his passion.

Raventhorpe was apologizing for having doubted my Arabella's love. "My darling girl, I have been wrestling my demons over what you told me this evening. I find I must believe you, because sacrificing yourself for me is exactly what you *would* do. What can I say, what can I do to make up for centuries of mistrust? How you must despise me! You surrendered your life for me, and I a very Judas."

"But I am not Arabella," I murmured, to ease my conscience.

"Then I am not Raventhorpe." He smiled, disbelieving. "Is it not time we two strangers knew one another more intimately?" he said softly. I let the hushed silence be my answer. If he took it for permission...

The lips seeking mine were no strangers. The past was past, yet lived again in us. This love was unquenchable. It had not died, but like some forgotten, primitive seed, had survived in the bosom of the earth, waiting its season to swell and burst forth. I could not hold myself back; I was drawn into the vortex of his passion by an elemental force of nature. The paramount force, overriding all others, to ensure man's survival. Sun and earth and dew swelled the seed of desire within me, in that sunless chamber. Alexander had wandered the universe until he found me, and I must now be with him. Our time had come. It was more than a lover; it was love itself that lay with me.

I wrapped my arms tightly around his insubstantial body. It was not quite of solid, human substance, yet it seemed to have some density now. There was more than the enveloping warmth; there was a demanding pressure against my flesh. But really the physical details were less important than the tide of pure love that raged about us, inundating mere rational thought. I felt Arabella's spirit was inhabiting me, and I gladly surrendered my body to her for these few brief moments, for which she had waited several lifetimes. Her lonely wanderings in the meadow would be rewarded at last.

"Say you don't despise me, my love. Say you forgive me," he urged.

"No, no. I don't despise you. I love you,

Alexander. I have always loved you. I was so sorry I hadn't gone to Gretna Green with you. I should have. I wanted so much to tell you how much I loved you that last night, but I dared not, with Sir Giles at my back with a pistol. I gladly died rather than have to marry William." There, I had said it, I had fulfilled her dying wish.

"My dear heart." His fevered lips traced nibbling arabesques on my throat; his voice was drugged with passion. The same feelings raged within me. "I am humbled by your love, but I wish you had not done it. My survival was no pleasure. It was hell on earth."

"But you knew a great many women!" I reminded him.

"I tried to fathom your treachery through a great many women. Hundreds of them, women without counting, but all with your face, when I closed my eyes. I wanted to hurt you, Belle, as you hurt me, and knew that violating our love was the way to do it. I regret every abandoned moment of that life, my own dear love. Most of all I regret that I scribbled it all down to mock you, and me, and make us infamous. What I really wanted was just to have you back as we used to be. So happy, and we didn't even know it." Regret echoed in his soft voice.

"We'll be happy again," I promised rashly.

Hungry kisses were rained on my eyes, my nose, my lips. In my ear he softly whispered, "You should have let me die with you, and we would have been together forever. I shouldn't mind eternity, if I could spend it with you."

"We are together now, my own dear heart," I breathed on a trembling sigh.

When he replied, his voice was hoarse with emotion. "They'll never tear us apart again," he said, then gave me his lips, and I claimed them for my own in a kiss that healed the age-old wounds that went beyond mere jealousy to touch the very depths of despair, and quicken it with hope.

I was suffocated with a delirium of passion. Blood pounded mercilessly in my ears as his warm fingers explored the intimate corners of my being, awakening me to unknown raptures. His warm hands measured the swells of my hips, then brushed higher to palm my breasts. His head lowered, and I felt the smooth roughness of his cheeks pressing into their yielding softness, as if he would like to drown there. Surges of pleasure washed through me. I folded him in my arms, savoring the strength of his stretching muscles, curving around me.

I had found the other half of myself—no! My other self had found me, and now we would be one. From all the tractless infinity of time and space he had found me. Like the shark drawn by the atomy of blood, he had sensed I was here, at this place, at this time, and had kept a rendezvous with destiny. For one brief hour, we outwitted Fate, and were together.

Our love gave meaning to the chaos that was life. We were the reason for it as well as the means. This was why so many dark nights had been endured, so many tears shed, so much blood spilt—for this brief instant of perfection. We were not of this world, but a spark to light the skies of eternity. From the vertiginous heights of the heavens I looked down on Belle Savage. Seeing her with my heart, I could only pity the hollowness that had been her existence.

My whole body was pierced with an ephemeral, shuddering joy, even while I knew it could not last. Its very brevity made it more precious. Such raging fires were not meant to endure. They burn themselves out like a dying star in one great convulsive streak across the sky, then scatter their sparks, which turn to ash as they settle on the ground. But to have known such a moment of glory—who could deny herself the miracle?

After the fullness of love, we lay back exhausted, still in each other's arms. "It was hell to come here." He smiled a drugged smile of satisfaction. "But it was worth it, my Belle. A never-to-be-forgotten night, a night to turn the gods green with envy."

I gazed on his beloved face, trying to penetrate to his mind as he chatted on. "I have traveled a long way, not quite knowing why, but believing it had to do with revenge. But when I saw you that first night by the weir— remember? I knew it was not hatred that drove me. It was wanting to regain your love. Through you, I have achieved the miracle of a second innocence, sweeter than the first for knowing the hell I have escaped. Without darkness, there is no light. And without the bitterness, who can savor the sweet?

"When I boarded the ship at Bournemouth, the skies poured down a stygian pitch. I stood on deck, lifting my face to let the rain wash my tears. It would have been a relief to know you were already dead. That is how wretched I was that night. Hate filled my heart. I stood at the railing, trying to gather courage to plunge in and end it all. I did not think life could hold more horrors for me, but I was wrong. I made it worse by becoming a dissolute wretch, wallowing in debauchery. That was me, without you, Belle. You were my better half. Now I can be at rest. For if you, whom I wronged, can forgive me, who shall say me nay? You *do* forgive me? Say you do! Let me be shrived of this burden I carry."

I had often sensed that ineffable sadness in him. I felt guilty that I could not assuage it, but how could I mislead him? This was infinity, the great intelligence of the universe we were dealing with, and the whole truth must be told. "I am not Arabella," I said. "She was a relative. I feel she was here tonight; I am sure she forgives you."

He shook his head in tolerant amusement. "Oh, my poor vain jewel! Not Arabella? Would *I* be mistaken about such a thing? The hair, the face, are slightly different in this body, but you are you. It is mainly the soul I see; the soul has not changed. How can you doubt it?" My doubts faded at his words, and a glowing euphoria filled me with wonder. "Some part of you recognized me from the first moment, as I recognized you," he continued. "I have carried on this charade until you came to accept the truth, for I knew you would flee if you knew the whole. You tried to run away the first—no, the second time I found you. I had to—handle the phone."

"With a poltergeist. Who was he?"

"That was no poltergeist. In the passion of the moment—the dread that you would leave—some benevolent God allowed me an instant's power to stop you. You were more yielding by the weir, but then it is fraught with memories for us."

I gazed on him in wonder, with a joy radiating through me. I was not a mere impostor. I was Arabella, his Arabella. And as the beautiful truth took hold, he began to fade. He smiled at me lovingly, with ineffable sorrow, as if for the last time. I tried to hold on to him, but as I reached for him with a sobbing gasp, I found myself alone. A howl of outrage rose in my throat. I lacked the strength to utter it. I threw myself back on the pillows in despair.

It could not have been a dream! It was

real, the most real thing that had ever happened to me. I felt it was the only real thing I had ever known, the only thing that mattered, that I was Arabella Comstock, that Raventhorpe loved me, and I him. How could I go on alone? After such knowledge, how was I to endure the dregs of life without him? It was the loss of my parents all over again, magnified a thousand times.

I lay alone in that bed, still warm with love, remembering, reliving those golden moments. Why had he tortured me with this glimpse of what might have been, if he only meant to desert me? But it was unfair to blame Alexander. He had moved heaven and bent earth to find me. And now he was at peace. He would be taken to that heaven where the fulfilled spirits go for their reward, and I was bound in this mortal coil for another half century. It was intolerable! Everyone I loved was gone. What had I to live for?

I would not let the malice of time rob me of Alexander again. I should have let him die with me, he had said, and he was right. What had remained for him was only degradation on earth, and torment in the hereafter. And nothing remained for me without him. We could have been together all those years; we could be together now. It was only this body of mine that kept us apart. A single step kept me from joining him. Death would give us life together.

I rose up from the bed, knowing what I

must do. I would go to him; he would be waiting for me at the weir, as he had waited times out of mind. The wind would be rustling the leaves of the willow trees, and stir the serrated tops of towering pines, silhouetted in ebony against the silver sky. The crescent moon would ride high over the roof of Chêne Bay, and in May, the ground under the fruit trees would be white with fallen petals. "Spring snow," Alexander called them. The old excitement invaded me, warming my cheeks and sending the hot blood coursing through my veins.

He would open his arms, and I would run to them, to my beloved, there by the cascading water that threw its silver droplets into the air. We would admire it one last time, then together, hand in hand and unafraid, we would plunge into the depths of the cold, black water. Our spirits would rise from it like a phoenix, together at last, forever.

I went in a fever of excitement to snatch up a shawl, the same white one I wore when he came to me last night. Was it only hours ago? What if he was not there? What if he had already gone to his eternal rest? I must hurry, before heaven claimed him. What if he did not recognize me? Ah, but he would recognize my soul. I was his dear Arabella. It was weakness to hesitate. I picked up the shawl and tossed it about my shoulders. It fell to the floor. I picked it up again, and was aware of a fierce tugging at the other end, as if an invisible hand pulled it away.

He was here, and I spoke, although I could not see him. "I am going with you, Alexander. Wait for me at the weir."

The shawl was hurled to the floor. A wild gust of wind invaded the closed room, blowing the curtains and lifting the counterpane. Its force sent me reeling against a chair. It was the same skirling blast with which he had arrived at the séance, and changed my life forever. He had shown me I was Arabella, and his presence had recalled to me that long-ago story. But since I was Arabella, I was already dead, so what did it matter?

"I *will* go! I *will*! Don't try to stop me!"

I left the shawl and ran to the door. It banged shut as I reached it. I took the knob in my fingers and wrenched with all my might, but it would not budge. It seemed the benevolent gods were on Alexander's side once more, lending him power. The closet door blew open, hitting the wall behind it with a violent force.

"You don't love me!" I shouted into the empty room. "You don't want me to go to you. I hate you, Alexander." Tears streamed down my face, and I threw myself, sobbing, on the bed. I felt warm fingers stroking my hair, as if I were a baby. The echo of unspoken crooning sounds filled my head. When the tears had subsided I said, or perhaps only thought, "I don't know what you want of me. Why did you come back, if we are not to be together?"

"In the fullness of time, my Belle. Not like this. Human life is precious; live out your allotted span. I will be waiting for you, as I have waited all these years." I sensed that suicide would prevent me from joining him, who had gained peace. I was doomed to another lifetime of waiting.

I rose up from the bed and picked up the shawl. The room was quiet, but I knew that he was with me yet awhile, watching over me. He was leaving, but he was not gone yet. The closet door began to vibrate almost imperceptibly, but my awareness was preternaturally alert to any sign. I took the shawl to the closet and hung it up slowly, waiting for a further sign.

Alexander was there, close by, leading me to some discovery. I glanced about the room until my eyes met Arabella's toilet table. I went to it and drew open the drawers, one by one. The upper right drawer came out only partway, like her desk. I turned the porcelain knob, and the fake back fell forward, revealing a small book, bound in white kid. On the front in gold lettering were the words *Sonnets to a Lady*.

I took it back to the bed and opened it. On the flyleaf was the inscription: "To Arabella from Alexander, with love— *toujours*." I turned the page. The sonnets were familiar, but as I read them with Arabella's eyes and heart, their meaning grew and expanded, and filled me with peace. A theme of waiting for love ran through them. It was only the interval to her sixteenth birthday that he wrote of, but the words suggested a much longer wait, since every hour apart had seemed like months. They were full of love, and asked for patience, for a love that is worth having is worth waiting for, though Time itself seemed to stand still. It would come, in the fullness of time. The bright promise would find fulfillment, or why had God made the promise?

I fell asleep with the book in my fingers, and awoke in the morning still grasping it, as a token of the promise made. Alexander was gone. Gone for good, but he had left a part of himself with me, to see me through the next half century or so, until I could join him. What was a half century to us, who had waited this long?

And I still had a job to do. I must find my former body, and prove to the rest of the world what I already knew. That there had been no betrayal between us. Alexander had paid for his temporal sins, and found his second innocence. I wanted the world to know that, and clear his name. I also wanted the world to know I had never stopped loving him.

Chapter Twenty-three

I felt strangely disoriented when I arose, not quite sure which century I inhabited, but I was not tired. In fact I felt strangely regenerated. Mollie popped in on her way to work while I was lingering over my second cup of coffee, reliving the happiness of Alexander's final visit. I feared it would fade like a dream, and I wanted to store up the details for future consolation.

Mollie wore a dress of military color and cut, with a double row of brass buttons and epaulets on the big padded shoulders. Her spike heels were khaki to match the uniform.

"And how are you this morning, Belle?" she asked.

"I'm fine." I didn't tell her about Alexander's last visit. Some things are too precious to share.

"All systems are go on the dig," she announced. "Ivan called last night. He says it's okay to dig up the spinney, but he wants us to keep it as quiet as possible. We'd have teeny-boppers from here to London if his fans got hold of it. People pooh-pooh things like ghosts, but they come swarming around at the first hint of one."

"That's wonderful, Mollie. When can you get away from work? I'm assuming you'd like to be here."

"I wouldn't miss it for anything. I'll get right on to Henry. His time's more or less his own, and I don't have any appointments this aft, so let's make it about two-thirty."

"I'll be ready. Do you have time for coffee?"

"Not today, thanks. I'm showing a house at nine, the one you didn't take." She waved and teetered off on her high heels.

I could still not settle down to work, or anything else. It seemed impossible that the world was wagging out there, that people were manufacturing cars, buying and selling houses, washing dishes, constructing skyscrapers, making love, and war.

Henry Thorndyke phoned at ten to say he would be here at two-thirty, and to discuss what equipment was needed. As I had no shovels, he volunteered to bring a couple, along with some crowbars and smaller tools.

I spent a morning of mental readjustment, trying to get myself firmly back in the twentieth century to finish the job I had undertaken. Creative work was impossible, but I read over my manuscript, trying to decide how to handle the ending. I would not follow Raventhorpe to Italy and Greece. Those years of debauchery did not exist for me. That was not my Alexander, but a poor soul, demented by losing Arabella. The work had begun as Arabella's story, and it would end with her death. A brief epilogue just mentioning Raventhorpe's transmogrification to Vanejul, and the reason for it, would round off the work. That latter part of his life was well chronicled, for those who were interested in it.

I changed into jeans and another of Dad's old shirts, smiling to myself to think how Alexander would dislike the jeans. How, in future, all my little actions would be haunted by the memory of his likes and dislikes. Henry and Mollie arrived together at two-thirty, Mollie in sneakers and jeans that were not kind to her figure, yet she wore her clothes with a panache that made them acceptable, and even attractive. Mollie had explained the whole story to Henry; he accepted it without question. In fact, he looked at me with a new respect and camaraderie. I didn't tell either of them that I was Arabella, however. They might have believed me; I don't know, and in any case, it didn't matter. I knew it was so.

We got the tools and a blanket from the back of Henry's truck and began the trek to the spinney. Up the hill past the whispering weir, with the sun shining in a Wedgwood blue sky and the birds wheeling overhead, along the path into the woods, to the clearing by the old oak tree.

"That's the place," I said, pointing to the stone.

"It'll take some leverage to pry that monster free," Henry said. "It certainly took more than one man to put it there."

I thought Sir Giles must have helped Robinson. He would not have wanted anyone else to know what it concealed. I wondered if he had ever told William the true story.

Henry oversaw the operation, and put his back into the job as well. We dug three holes along one side of the rock, pushed our crowbars in as far under it as possible, and heaved. It was a long, hard, heavy job. Our arms were aching and our brows were dripping before we were done, but eventually the rock rolled over, and a scattering of insects fled from the light. After we had rested a moment, we began digging with the shovels. The earth was dry, pale brown, and surprisingly soft.

"Dig carefully," Henry said. "We don't want to disturb the bones."

I thought of Shakespeare's gravestone.

Good friend, for Jesus sake forbeare
To digg the dust encloased heare

Arabella was not much further removed in time from Shakespeare than from our present generation. It seemed truly incredible that we were about to see a body that had been interred so long ago. Yet I hadn't a single doubt in my mind that we would see her remains. Nor did I entertain any thought that we would be cursed for our efforts. This is what she wanted. I would try to get the present Lord Raventhorpe to have her buried beside Alexander in their family plot, where his remains had eventually found their final resting place, when they were brought back from Greece. That would round out the circle as they would both like.

Sir Giles had buried his sins deep. There were four feet of earth covering the mortal remains. The skeleton of a hand was the first thing uncovered. We switched to trowels and worked with extreme care. The other hand lay beside the first. Neither hand wore a ring. She had removed the band of diamond baguettes William had given her before going to meet Raventhorpe that fatal night. As the skull appeared, I moved the earth away gently with my fingers. Henry handed me a soft whisk to remove the last of the clinging earth.

Her golden hair was completely gone. A hideous grinning skull stared back at me across the centuries. The cavities that had been her eyes were holes, filled with the soft, dun-colored earth. Her teeth, still intact, were the more frightening thing. Their curved shape suggested a rictuslike grin. The flesh had dwindled to a flaky brown substance that clung to the bones. When I saw the discolored pearls lying in the earth where her ears once were, I knew this had been Arabella. They were the same teardrop pearls she wore in Thorndyke's portrait at Chêne Bay.

We were all silent, gazing at the skull, thinking our own thoughts. I had thought I would feel as if I were at my own funeral, but it wasn't like that. I felt strangely detached. There was a terrible aching sadness in the air, but I had already lived through the outrage and desecration of it all, and come to terms with it. Now I must get on with the job of moving these bones to rest beside Alexander's.

"You were right, Belle," Mollie said quietly.

Henry said, "Those are the eardrops she wore in the picture my ancestor painted. We'll leave them. It will help prove who she is. We'll leave her just as we found her and let the experts do the moving."

"Yes, we'll leave her just as she is," I replied, as he was looking to me for instructions. "I want those experts to see if they can find the bullet that killed her. It should be there, under the ribs. Now, who should we call, Henry? The police, I suppose. Will Ivan mind, Mollie?"

"The police won't let the hordes come in. That's all he's concerned about. I'll phone him, though. He mentioned his uncle would want to know. Professor Thumm—he wrote a book about Vanejul and Arabella."

I disliked to hear Alexander called Vanejul. "Ivan is Professor Thumm's nephew?" I asked, wondering at such disparate talents in one family.

"Yes, his mum's older brother. That's how Ivan got interested in Chêne Bay in the first place. His uncle wanted to buy it, but of course, he couldn't afford it."

"I thought Professor Thumm would be dead by now," I said.

"No, he's an active seventy. He wrote that book when he was fresh down from Oxford. He's written dozens of historical biographies since then. He might arrange to have an archaeologist from the university come along to look at the body, and remove it carefully."

"That's a good idea."

Henry remained with the body while Mollie and I went to Chêne Mow to call the police. She also called Ivan, who had no objection to our plan, and said he would join us as soon as possible. He said his uncle would certainly want to come as well. Ivan would notify him.

There was a great deal of excitement at Chêne Bay over the next few days. Reporters and TV newsmen descended on us. Dr. Thumm did indeed have archaeologists and other experts examine the find. The bullet was recovered, as I hoped. I was questioned as to why I suspected Arabella was buried in the spinney.

"Call it an intuition," I said vaguely. I did not announce that I was Arabella. That was not the point of the story. "I've been studying the history of Arabella and Raventhorpe for a book I'm writing. Mrs. Millar found some of Raventhorpe's letters to Arabella in a desk she got from Chêne Bay. They led me to suspect Sir Giles Throckley of the murder. Since the body was never found in the weir, I felt he must have buried it on the estate. It was a process of elimination. It would have been buried in some secluded spot, to avoid accidental detection."

"You're writing a book?" one of the reporters asked. "When will it be published?"

"I haven't finished it yet, but I hope the publisher who did my first novel will be interested in it."

When the interview was aired, I had several calls from publishers and editors, including Anne Morrissey from Crowley. She was surprised at my change of direction, but interested. We arranged a mutually satisfactory deal. Anne also asked about *Rebel Heart*. I felt some eagerness to be getting on with it, too. I had my hero now. There would be some trace of Alexander in all my heroes for a long time to come. The physical details would change, of course, but his passion was heroic. That was the necessary item for a hero.

Chapter Twenty-four

There was so much commotion at Chêne Mow that it was impossible to get on with my writing. I sublet the cottage and rented a room at Emily Millar's. Beezle was happy to get home. I wanted to stay in the New Forest to finalize the book, there where it all happened.

Emily, as usual, was very helpful. She gave permission to publish the letters, and even allowed me to keep the locket, which I never remove. I keep it on me constantly, as some brides refuse to remove their wedding rings.

"It belongs to you," she said, with her secret smile.

"You know, don't you, Emily?" I said hesitantly.

"That you are Arabella? I always suspected it," she replied. "Did you notice, at the May Day séance, how the whirlwind that brought Raventhorpe rushed all around the circle, then straight to you? When we discovered the spirit was Raventhorpe, I began to suspect who you were."

"I didn't notice. It was all so strange and frightening."

"It was a new experience for you, dear," she said forgivingly. "Mollie told me you had some familiarity with Chêne Mow. Then when you came to me, so curious about Arabella, and so eager to have the locket... Let us just say it felt right, if you're uncomfortable with clairvoyance."

"I'm not uncomfortable with it. How could I be, now?"

"Clairvoyance just means clear vision. Nowadays people don't see clearly. They only look with their eyes. You have to use your heart, too. The name Belle was a curious coincidence, and there were the family records from Chêne Mow. One thing led to another. When did you come to realize it yourself, Belle?"

"Not until he told me—Alexander. He recognized my soul."

"That would be it, of course." She nodded. "There's not much resemblance in the face, though there is a little something. That pointed chin is pure Comstock."

Over the days, we had many conversations, and Emily told me her thoughts on life. We were in the garden, admiring the flowers one sunny afternoon.

"They're so beautiful, they seem a kind of miracle," I said, idly flicking a pure white rose that nodded in the sun.

"They're part of the miracle of life," she said. "We're all part of it. The mystery is all around us, and especially within us. We are like the flowers. The seed of new life is released in the death of the old. Dear me, I'm raving. Pay no heed to the ramblings of an old lady."

Over tea one afternoon, we talked about the present Lord Raventhorpe. Selecting a Fig Newton, Emily said, "I had hoped that Adam might be Alexander reincarnated and fall in love with you, Belle—he's a bachelor. But that was too much to hope."

"I wondered myself. We met a motorcycle head-on that day, on the bus coming here from Stratford. The driver seemed to stop and stare right at me. He nearly hit the bus. Then I heard on television that Lord Raventhorpe's accident occurred that same day near Stratford."

"And Alexander appeared at about the time Adam was in coma. Yes, that looked extremely fortuitous. Just one of those coincidences, I daresay. I expect you'd like to meet him before you leave England?"

"That would be nice. Do you think the Raventhorpes would let Arabella be buried in their family plot?"

"I'll ask Lily, Lady Raventhorpe. She is back at Oldstead with Adam now. He was having bouts of coma, but is recovering nicely. The Throckleys will be glad to be spared the bother of the burial. They're old, you know, and in Portugal—enjoying *your* money," she added with a sniff, as if the crime were of recent vintage. The English have long memories.

I used to take my afternoon break from writing in Emily's lovely garden. After coming to know her better, I found myself viewing the world with a keener eye. I felt its mysteries in my blood, as though every sense were preternaturally acute. The sky looked bluer, the grass a hundred shades of green. Each blade had its own life. At such moments, I truly felt a part of nature, connected by an invisible power to the whole world.

Lord Raventhorpe, of keen interest to me because of his kinship with Alexander, agreed to have Arabella's mortal remains interred beside Alexander. He sent me a letter that had something of Alexander's charm and insouciance. He wrote:

Dear Belle—
May I call you Belle? After having seen you on the telly so often recently, I feel I know you already. I am charmed by your interest in my infamous relation. Of course Arabella must be buried beside her fiancé. But for an accident of fate, she would be a Raventhorpe. You make

me feel culpable for not having taken the matter in hand myself. It seems like Providence that, although the family graveyard is quite crowded, there is one empty plot on the left side of Alexander's grave. No one could tell me why it had been left vacant. Now we know who it has been waiting for, all those years.

He continued with the time and place of the interment, and ended, "Of course you will come. I look forward with the greatest anticipation to meeting you, and thanking you on behalf of my late cousin. *Adieu,* Raventhorpe."

The letter had been done on a word processor and printer, so that I had only his signature to judge his handwriting, but its flourishing, bold strokes were not unlike my Alexander's.

The ceremony took place on a sunny morning in early June. I felt Alexander was looking on to see how things turned out. I could almost hear him scolding. "Damme, about time you got here, woman!"

I was pleased to see that Lord Raventhorpe had chosen a white marble headstone to match Alexander's. It bore a simple inscription: Arabella's name and dates, and "Betrothed to Lord Raventhorpe." Beneath it he had added the inscription on the back of the locket, the single word, *"Toujours."* How did he know? I had not told that to anyone who interviewed me. But of course, Emily was a relative; I assumed she had told him. In any case, it was exactly the right epitaph.

Besides a hundred newsmen and cameras, a large contingent from Lyndhurst attended the burial. Mollie, in a dark balloon gown and a wide-brimmed black feathered hat; Emily in a sedate blue dress; Henry Thorndyke; and Sappho in a very elegant gown of unrelieved black with a veil covering her face. She said she had decided not to write about Arabella and Raventhorpe. She was researching Emma Hamilton and Admiral Nelson instead.

The sun shone on the open grave before us and the gravestone there beside it. It seemed incredible that Alexander's marble headstone should be worn smooth on the edges, with moss creeping up the sides. His death seemed so recent to me. Arabella's stone would look garishly new beside it. But with the passing of the centuries, hers, too, would be smoothed by the hand of time. Wind and rain would soften its sharp edges, until the two stones appeared coeval.

Adam—I have saved the best for the last—was still using a cane after his accident. He was not an exact reincarnation of Alexander, but the resemblance was striking. He was tall and well formed, with black hair and those same sloeberry eyes as my beloved. It seemed impossible that the family characteristics had continued so strongly over so many years. He looked aristocratically elegant in a formal gray morning coat and top hat. When he removed the hat for the burial, the sunlight struck his hair, glinting rainbows off its sable smoothness. His expression was sober rather than sad.

He came forward and stood beside me during the ceremony. When it was time to throw the handful of earth on the coffin, he put his cane under his arm and held my hand with his free one. He didn't speak, but just looked in such a familiar way that I felt I had known him before—that I had known him forever. When it was over, he turned to me as if we were old friends and said, "You will come up to the house now, Belle. You will want to see some of Alexander's things. Damme, this busted wing holds me back."

"Where did your accident happen?" I said, half-afraid to ask the question.

He cocked his head in a way I had often seen Alexander do and replied, "You don't remember? Tsk tsk. Let me refresh your memory, my pet. I saw this beautiful woman—what else would make me lose my head at such a perilous moment?—on a bus just outside of Stratford. She looked demmed familiar. I didn't see the lorry coming half a block away. Is it coming back to you at all?"

I felt faint, as if the blood were rushing from my head. "It was you!"

He just went on looking in a way that answered my question. "Not the optimum spot for our reunion, but beggars can't be choosers. I want to show you the letters Arabella wrote to Alexander. I've saved them for you all these years."

"You've only known of me for a few weeks."

"A little longer than that," he said, softly smiling. "A century or two. It's seemed a couple of millennia. We have a lot of lost time to make up."

"I don't mind waiting," I said in a weak, disbelieving voice.

Again his eyes met mine in a spine-tingling way. His lips curved in a smile that accentuated his resemblance to Alexander. There was knowledge in his gaze, and impatience, and love. "No, what are a few more moments to us, eh, Belle? We are experts at waiting."

In that instant, I knew beyond doubt the enchanted boundary had opened, and by some kind intervention of providence, I had found him again. This time nothing would keep us apart.

If you have enjoyed reading this large
print book and you would like more infor-
mation on how to order a Wheeler Large
Print Book, please write to:

 Wheeler Publishing, Inc.
P.O. Box 531
Accord, MA 02018-0531